BATTLE EARTH IV

NICK S. THOMAS

First published in the United Kingdom in Feb 2012 by Swordworks Books.

ISBN 978-1-909149-00-7

Typeset by Swordworks Books
Printed and bound in the UK & US
A catalogue record of this book is available from the British Library

Cover design by Swordworks Books
www.swordworks.co.uk

BATTLE EARTH IV

NICK S. THOMAS

PROLOGUE

War had raged for little over nine months with the alien invaders before they were driven from Earth. In the pages of human history it had been a short war, but all that had witnessed it were left forever changed. The Ares research base on Mars was the first target. The Lunar colony, the largest human colony outside of Earth's atmosphere had been next. The survivors of the five hundred thousand Moon colonists had fled below ground to continue to wage a guerrilla war.

Spain and North Africa had quickly fallen. France had been the bastion of Europe, but now lay in ruins. South America had fallen, and North America had barely held the line. Soldiers from all around the globe fought alongside one another to save their planet.

Major Taylor's heroic defeat of the enemy leader Karadag had caused the enemy armies to flee the planet, but they were far from finished. The deaths of Captain Friday and so many other comrades weighed heavily on Chandra's Company, and no one could yet believe that the war could be over.

The enemy army loomed over Earth from their retreat on the Lunar colony. Nobody knew their intentions, but it was clear they were not ready to leave.

CHAPTER ONE

"To our fallen friends!" yelled Taylor.

He lifted his glass above his head in a salute. The crowd around the table on which he was stood roared in appreciation as glasses clashed together. He lifted the container to his lips and threw back the beer so that it trickled out of the sides and down his chin. He wiped his mouth and looked around as he gazed at the festivities.

Mitch could feel the fatigue in his drooping eyes. He wanted nothing more than to have it all stop and to settle down for some much needed rest. But the hard days of work were only broken up by hard partying. He staggered as he lowered himself down onto a stool and finally to the floor. Mitch landed hard and swayed a few steps over into Sergeant Silva who turned and smiled.

"Easy there, Major," he jested.

Mitch righted himself and took another swig from his

beer. He turned to have Eli rush at him and launch her tongue down his throat. She tasted of Vodka and was drunker than him. Neither of them cared anymore for hiding their feelings and relationship. It was such common knowledge that nobody hassled them over it.

"When are we going home?" she asked.

He shook his head and shrugged his shoulders in response.

"Oh, come on, we gonna be here forever?"

"What are you so desperate to get back to?"

She looked at him puzzled. "Home, what else?"

"I'm not sure I'd recognise it anymore," he mused.

She shook her head, not understanding what he meant.

"The war didn't reach our homes," she stated.

"It's not that. It's us that have changed. Do we just go home and go back to our old lives?"

"Why not? We've been here long enough. Long enough for a lifetime."

He nodded to show he understood her, but he did not believe it. He caught a glimpse of Chandra approaching. She was pulling back a hood from her head, and her clothing was dripping wet.

"Evening, Major!" called Eli.

"I see you're making the most of the night," she replied.

Eli raised her shot glass in salute as she turned and left them to their business. They could both see that she had arrived to address Taylor.

"What is it?" he asked.

"Our work will be done here tomorrow. The locals who are returning will take it from here. We have orders to pack up and leave by noon."

"Where we heading?"

"Help the clear up at Reims."

"Christ, is this what we have become? Clearers and builders?"

She dipped her head and sighed. As much as both of them had wanted to see an end to the fighting, it was a long way from the future they had expected.

"France had some of the worst of it, you know that. It's our job to help return some normality to these people's lives. We'll do whatever we can to help."

"All that fighting, all the death, the loss? How much more can be asked of us?"

She hauled Mitch in close.

"A damn sight more. This war isn't over. It won't be over until every one of those sons of bitches is dead. We'll continue to do everything that is expected of us and more."

He nodded in agreement. Taylor felt some shame for having little compassion left for the civilians. They had become refugees, and their towns had been reduced to rubble while he still had a home to return to. But he could not help feel they had all given enough already.

"I'm going to get a drink and enjoy the rest of the

evening. Tomorrow we get a change of scenery, and that'll be a good thing. Keep it together for all of us, you hear?"

Taylor looked away for a moment as he took another drink and turned back to Chandra.

"We getting a lift to Reims?"

"That's more like it," she replied. "I have already organised for trucks and some engineering vehicles to join us. Sergeant Dubois was most helpful in convincing the General as such.

Taylor smiled as he turned and looked to the bar where the French Sergeant was sat. She was engulfed in conversation with Captain Jones whom she had her arm wrapped around. It brought a smile to his face to see the darkness that had grown in Jones being washed away. He was laughing for the first time in as long as either of them could remember.

"You see that?" asked Chandra. "Amongst all this pain and suffering, and the near obliteration of our race, and yet that is hope. Humans will always seek to find some good in every situation, and it's something you should remember, Major."

He nodded in agreement. All he ever wanted was to see an end to the war and be able to relax and enjoy the company of friends in peace, but in the back of his mind, he knew it was not to last.

"You know I thought you'd like helping to clear and rebuild. It's a walk in the park after what we've been through."

He turned and looked up into her eyes. He wondered for a moment if she really liked the peace they had won. She seemed anxious to get back to combat.

"It's what we wanted, an end to it all. But it's not quite the triumphant celebrations I had envisaged. Toiling over desolate waste grounds that we have already bled over and lost so many good friends."

"It won't last forever," she replied.

"There's still a lot of work to be done."

"Yeah, proper soldiering though."

"The damn war's over, Major, can't you leave it be?"

He slammed down his glass and turned away from Chandra. She was left speechless at the bar as she was handed a drink. *Can't blame him*, she thought. *He's had it tougher than most.*

Taylor pushed his way through the troops to look for Eli, but he stopped as he recognised an old officer enter the bar in front of him. The face was just a little familiar, but he could not place it. The man must have been close to sixty but was in good shape. His face was scarred and weathered. He held himself high and proud.

On the man's arm was the faded symbol of the Moon Defence Force. Either side of him stood younger men of the same army. He could already tell that they recognised him.

"Fuck," he said under his breath.

He remembered his first encounter with the enemy on the Moon colony, and the mission they had carried out. No MDF soldier would have fond memories of that time. Taylor had his orders, and that didn't involve assisting the colonists.

"Major Taylor," he spat with a dour face.

Mitch shook his head. He could already tell it was not a situation he needed right now.

"How you doing, fellas?" he responded.

"Still standing, no thanks to you."

He remembered the man's commanding voice. Then it came back to him, the MDF Commander Kelly, who he had met during the rescue of the Prime Minister. *Ah shit,* he thought.

"Another time, alright?" he asked.

Taylor took a few steps to go past them, but one of the MDF soldiers shuffled along to block his path.

"Let him be!" Kelly ordered.

The despondent soldier glared into Taylor's eyes before the Commander shouted his command a little louder.

"Lieutenant Perera, step aside!"

Taylor didn't remember ever meeting the younger officer, but he could see the hatred in the man's eyes.

Perera moved aside and watched Mitch like a hawk as he avoided eye contact and shuffled on towards the restrooms. *Jeez,* thought Taylor. *Save the fucking world and they're still not happy.*

As he stood relieving himself, he thought back to his last battle. The killing of Karadag should have been an event to celebrate for years to come, but it did not bring the satisfaction he sought.

The doors swung open behind him, and he caught a glimpse of Jones staggering in to stand at the receptacle beside him. The Captain had a delirious grin on his face and was drunk enough to have forgotten the horrors he had seen for just a while.

"We moving out?" he slurred.

"That's right. To Reims."

"They got better beer there?"

Taylor chuckled.

"Captain Reyes reckons he can score a few kegs of English ale for us. I told him you might be interested."

Jones turned and looked in amazement.

"No shit?"

"Hey, if it can be done, I'll have it."

"Feels could to kick back and enjoy life a bit, don't you think?"

Taylor thought for a moment before mumbling in agreement. He couldn't think of a town or a country he even wanted to be. All he wanted was Eli and to leave it all behind. He loved the Company and all the friendship within it. But their faces reminded him every day of all those he would never see again.

"The Major believes the Krycenaeans are far from

gone," said Taylor.

"Ah fuck it, they're not here now, are they?"

Taylor smiled. He'd never seen the British Captain be so vulgar and casual. It was a relief to see life return to his eyes. It made him wonder why he felt so down. Jones had been through all he had and worse, and yet was in a better place emotionally.

"How do you do it?" asked Mitch.

"What?"

"Put all this behind you and move forward?"

Jones grimaced as he thought back to his horrifying experience as a prisoner of the invaders. He tried to smile through it, but Taylor could see the pain still burning inside.

"There's nothing else to do, is there? You can wallow in it all and become a head case like I did, or man the fuck up."

Taylor's eyebrow lifted as he turned his head and looked at his old friend in surprise. For a moment he had sounded like the forever cool headed Captain Friday. It was a sad reminder of the loss of one good friend, but a pleasant experience to see the return of another. Jones stepped past and patted him on the back.

"Come on, Mitch, this ain't half bad. War's over, and we can finally enjoy ourselves a little."

Taylor finished up and strode over to the washbasins as Jones left the room. He cupped water from the tap and splashed it over his face. The cool clear water instantly gave him a wake up kick. He breathed in deeply as he tried to relax and settle down. For all the time he had wanted to see the war end, having to confront a new life of peace was more difficult than he expected.

He walked past the drier and shook his hands off as he stepped back out into the bar. Within a few metres, he was once again stopped by one of the MDF servicemen. Lieutenant Perera stood before him with an angry face and a bottle held at its neck by his side. Taylor shook his head. He only wanted to return to Eli and enjoy the rest of the evening.

"Come on, man, give me a break," Taylor snarled.

"You were there when it all began. You were there and could have helped," replied Perera. "Where were you when our people were butchered, and we fled for our lives?" he spat.

Taylor shook his head in astonishment. He couldn't help but feel that after everything he had done, he didn't owe the man anything. He looked down away from the Lieutenant's angry eyes and could not find any words to utter.

"The deaths of our people are on you! You could have helped!"

Mitch could feel the anger brewing inside as he was being condemned for not saving the lives of people he could never have helped. Perera stood tall in front of him and awaited an answer. Finally, Taylor looked up and stared into his eyes. A frown grew in his face as his tolerance of the man seeped away.

"I have done everything in my power to save as many lives as possible. Why don't you take some fucking responsibility and stop acting like a pussy?" growled Taylor.

Perera's face went red with anger, and he took a wild and uncontrolled hook for Mitch's face. The Major was a little dulled by the alcohol but no more so than the Lieutenant. He ducked under the strike and drove an uppercut into the man's stomach. As the man reeled in pain, he yanked him back upright and drove a push kick into his torso that threw Perera back across the room and tumbling into several other MDF soldiers.

Before Taylor could marvel at his work, he felt a sharp pain as a punch connected with the side of his jaw. His stumbled a few paces before regaining his balance. Kelly stood there with his guard up and firmly ready to defend his colleague.

"Get 'em!" shouted Monty.

The bar burst into action as a melee erupted. Taylor was rushed by two of the Moon soldiers who came between him and Kelly and tackled him to the ground. He struggled to get them off but was trapped under their weight. He punched up into the flank of one to soften him up, and the man yelped in pain but did not move. He lifted his knee and smashed it into the same man's chest that made him gasp for air. The other punched him hard in the face. His head bounced off the ground, and his vision blurred for a moment. He gritted his teeth and thrust upward, striking the man on the edge of his chin. His head recoiled backwards but quickly recovered.

Taylor struggled to get free but could not get out of the grasp of the two men who stubbornly refused to move, no matter how much he softened them up. Out of the corner of his eye, he saw Jones rush across the room and launch one of the men across the room with a brutal kick. Mitch cut down with a knife hand to the other man's collar, quickly incapacitated him. Jones hauled Mitch to his feet, and they looked around for their next targets.

"Can't take you anywhere," Jones smiled.

Over a dozen soldiers were engaged in an all out battle across the bar with others joining in as it spread. Jones turned to face off against an incoming bunch as Taylor squared up against his next opponent. The MDF soldier before him was a woman, a fact that made him hesitate for a moment. She saw the opening and jabbed him hard to the face, and blood burst from his nose. He turned back with a smile as the blood gleamed on his teeth, her feistiness amusing him.

The woman thrust another strike forwards, but Taylor voided it and took a hold on her arm, wrenching her forward. As she was launched off her feet towards him, he drove a knee into her stomach and quickly followed it with a left to the jaw that knocked her to the ground. He looked up with a smile to revel in the destruction but was met with a snooker cue being wrapped around his face.

Taylor staggered back and tripped over the woman's body, landing hard on his back. The cue had snapped and splintered off. The impact had been taken on his left cheek and side of his head, momentarily disorientating him. He got to his feet and took a wild swing at another soldier that sent them both off balance and the other man flat on his face to the floor.

He turned around and swayed to one side causing him to stagger and fall into a table. He could feel blood trickling down his face and more than a little dizzy. Sirens rang out from outside the building, quickly followed by the cries of the Military Police as they rushed into the complex with stun batons. He ducked under a strike from one of the batons and hit the officer with an uppercut to his gut. The man folded and collapsed down.

Taylor turned to face another but was hit full force in the back of the knee by a baton. The Major stumbled to get to his feet but was thrust with one of the electrified batons and pushed to the ground. He remembered shaking from the voltage before being struck in the head and knocked unconscious.

* * *

Taylor awoke in a small pool of his own blood and saliva. He was face down on a hard concrete floor. He rolled onto his side and rubbed his eyes as he tried to regain composure and focus. As he began to get his sight back, he could make out cell bars a metre in front. It was a grim reminder of his incarceration, and he leapt up to his feet. He turned to see several other bloodied soldiers sharing the cell with him. He recognised the brothers, Monty and Blinker.

Opposite them were sat Commander Kelly and three of his troops. They looked up at him but showed no aggression. Despite the pain in his body, he felt remarkably sober. He must have been out for some time.

"How you doing, Major?" asked Blinker.

Taylor turned away from the Commander to look at the two friendly faces.

"Still standing, how long we been here?"

"Few hours," replied Monty.

"Guess they aren't too keen on a little friendly disagreement?"

The two brothers chuckled.

"You got us in here, Major," muttered Kelly. "Think you can get us back out?"

Taylor turned around to see that the MDF Commander was not joking. Blood had dried where it had poured from the man's mouth. He was stern and confident but not confrontational.

"It was your boy that started this. Striking a superior officer, that's a serious offence."

"Ah, hell, what does it matter anymore? We just need to get out of this shithole."

"It matters to me. We have given everything in this war, and I don't appreciate having the efforts of my Company brought into question by an officer who wasn't even here."

Kelly nodded in agreement.

"Look, I get it. I have seen the reports. I know what you and your people have done."

"No, you don't," interrupted Taylor. "You weren't there. You think you can have any idea of what we went through by reading a few notes?"

Kelly nodded in agreement once again.

"I get it, Major, I really do. We cannot know what you went through, but we didn't sit this war out either. We were prisoners in our own colony. We had nowhere to run. We were waking up every day and expecting it to be our last. Do you know what it feels like to live within a siege? When you know that if the defences fail, everyone dies. Every soldier, every civilian, all the children."

Kelly stopped for a minute to take in a deep breath and calm him. "Our war was no walk in the park is all I am saying."

"I never said it wasn't, but I didn't look for a fight back there," snapped Taylor.

Taylor turned and paced back across the room.

"I am not saying what Lieutenant Perera did was right. I'm just saying that under such extreme pressure, we don't always make the best decisions. We've lost our home colony and a great deal of our friends. I will discipline him appropriately."

Taylor strolled over to Monty and took a seat beside him on the hard and uncomfortable bench that ran the length of the wall.

"You should know that I never wanted to leave your colony back then. I wanted to help you, but I had no choice."

Kelly sighed. "I know. None of us could have foreseen this was the way it was gonna go. Who could have known we would ever have to face such an enemy in our lifetimes? Hell, in our history?"

"We made it though, didn't we?" replied Taylor. "We're still standing."

"True, but many aren't. All we ever wanted was to be left alone on our colony. We thought the threat upon us came from Earth, from corporations and governments wanting to muscle in on what we had. Never could we have imagined that we'd have to flee our homes."

"You really like it up there that much? Living in artificial environments?"

"It was our land. Few Earthers ever understood."

"No, I get it. A man will defend what is his to the very end, no matter how little it may seem in the face of others.

But now you have a chance to rebuild your community here on Earth. Hell, there's certainly some space going free."

"It's not a pleasant thought to be filling a space where a population has been exterminated," he replied.

The cell went silent as they all thought about it for a moment.

"By that thought, we'd never live anywhere. Humans have butchered each other for as long as we have lived, and wherever you are, you stand over bloodied ground."

"Maybe that's why we liked the Moon. We started from afresh," replied Kelly.

Doors opened down the corridor and footsteps approached. Moments later, Commander Phillips appeared with an MP on either side. No one in the cell uttered a word.

"Major Taylor, it seems you are adamant to get back behind bars. Commander Kelly, I was surprised to see your name on the list of those detained during this disturbance."

"It was a soldier's disagreement, nothing more."

"I trust it has now been resolved?"

The two officers nodded in agreement.

"Good. We have seen enough conflict over the last year, so how about we work together from now on? I can put this down to a little too much drink and a one off incident, but Gentlemen, do not let it happen again. The

French authorities are trying to rebuild their country, and the last thing they need is trouble. You're all here to help rebuild, not destroy what's left."

"Understood, Sir," replied Taylor.

"Major Chandra informs me that you are moving out at noon. I have procured release for all of you, on the condition that you will all return immediately to your billets and sleep off this silliness."

"Much appreciated, Sir. You won't see any more trouble from us."

"See that I don't."

The MPs stepped forward and opened the doors of the cell. The soldiers sat on both sides of the room sighed as they stood up and worked their aching muscles and joints. Kelly stood before Taylor.

"We don't blame you for not helping us. You have become famous for your deeds down here to save Earth, but you can't help some of my lads feeling a little put out."

"I was only following orders," replied Taylor.

Kelly nodded. "I know. Sometimes orders are the best thing to do, but not the right thing. I know you have some experience of this."

Taylor smiled in response, and Phillips laughed at the sentiment. Taylor had breached his orders more than any man could ever expect to get away with.

"You look after yourself, Major," said Kelly as he strolled out of the cell.

"Go home, Major, enjoy what sleep you can get before dawn."

Home? He wasn't sure he had one any longer. The company of Eli seemed to be the comfort and security a home might offer, and it was the best thing he could hope for. He stepped forwards and out of the cell. In the corridor, he found the other doors open and the rest of the troops being released. Eli stood awaiting him with a bruised jaw.

"You just couldn't stay out of it, could you?" he asked.

She smiled in response.

"Hey, it's been years. After the battles we've been through, it was nice to have a fair fight for a change."

He threw his arm over her shoulder, and she wrapped hers around his waist. He winced as he felt new bruises on his flank where someone must have kicked him on the ground after he'd been knocked unconscious.

"You okay?" she asked.

"This? It's nothing."

She didn't press him any further. Taylor had been through far worse beatings and didn't need to be reminded of it. The bloodied soldiers staggered back to their billets. It was a pleasant reminder of some of the good nights out they had enjoyed before the war had begun, but the locals didn't seem to agree. Civilians continued to pour into the country day and night. Vehicles rolled past that were packed to the roof while others walked back to their homes.

"What are they even going home to?" asked Eli.

"Whatever is left, it's still their homes, where else are they supposed to go?" replied Taylor.

Police sirens rang out as MPs tried to weave through the heavy traffic and clogged paths. Many roads were still not clear of debris, and some no longer existed. Much travelling had to be done by military vehicles and the few civilian cross country vehicles that could be mustered.

"Think we'll be here much longer?"

Taylor sighed. "I guess not."

She stopped him and looked in surprise. "You don't want to go home?"

Taylor shook his head.

"This has become home, more so than ever. Does going home mean returning to lives we no longer know, and leaving behind so many we now call friends? Returning from where we came is not going home."

"Well that's pretty fucking cynical."

Taylor shrugged his shoulders. He could not help but feel disassociated with his old life. Victory had not been anything like he had hoped for. He knew he should be thankful for escaping any charges that night, but it was little relief. His head was swollen, and his worn and faded uniform soaked in fresh blood of his own. None of them spoke anymore on their return.

Mitch kicked open the door of his temporary shelter

and stumbled inside with Eli close behind. He winced as he pulled off his uniform. He was tired of the pain he felt physically and emotionally. Eli came close and wrapped her arms around him, but he had little care for it. He brushed her aside and climbed into bed. She could see the sadness in his eyes and did not pursue it. They lay side-by-side for a few moments until she realised neither were ready to sleep.

"Karadag..." she said.

"What of him?"

"We never discussed him."

"What is there to say? We left the bastard in a pool of his own blood."

"I know. What I meant was, there must surely be more like him? We have many Generals and many heroes in our armies."

Taylor stopped and thought for a moment. They had been so focused on taking down the enemy leader that the idea of others had passed him by. It was a depressing thought as he realised she was bound to be right.

"Maybe, but armies of Earth used to led by Kings, so maybe he was the same. When Alexander the Great died, his armies scattered to the wind. Same as Genghis Khan."

"That's wishful thinking," she muttered.

"Have we not suffered enough against them? Maybe they want this war to be over as much as we do?"

They both fell silent as they thought on that concept. It

was hard to imagine that the Krycenaeans could ever live in peace.

"Makes you think, doesn't it? If they exist, what else is in the universe? Are there whole other worlds?"

"That have already been conquered or obliterated by the Krycenaeans?" asked Taylor.

"Or something bigger and meaner?" she responded.

"All we ever wanted to do was reach the stars, and look where it has gotten us. Had we not gone to the Moon, to Mars, maybe they would never have found us," mused Taylor.

"And maybe they would have found us just the same, and they would have found a far less capable opponent. We survived this war by the skin of our teeth. We survived it because the human race always strives for more and better. What happened to you Mitch? Since the fighting ended, you've become a shell of your former self. Isn't this the peace you wanted?"

He grunted and lay silent.

"What more can we ask for?" she insisted.

"I can think of a lot. For this war to have never happened."

"And I am sure all that have seen such days they wished they had not, but we made it through."

She knew she wasn't getting through to him. She went silent and cuddled into his side in the hope of giving him some comfort. There was little time left until dawn, and as much as dire thoughts plagued Taylor's mind, he eventually succumbed to his exhaustion.

CHAPTER TWO

Taylor awoke with a blistering headache and looked across to see an empty bed. They worked hard every day to help restore some normality to the region, but it felt like a never-ending job. It was only broken up by an ever more tiring series of parties and intoxication. He sighed as he crawled out of bed and sat up. A cold breeze swept in from where the door was ajar. The snow of winter had already begun to set even in the busy streets. All of Eli's gear was gone, including her Reitech suit.

"Ah shit," he muttered.

He pulled on his gear and stepped out into the daylight. Most of the Company were sat under a dining shelter enjoying their breakfast.

"Hey, Major!" shouted Silva.

The Sergeant beckoned for Mitch to join him. Taylor strode over and could see that Jones, Chandra and Yorath all sat together. A seat was left empty with a full plate of food placed next to it.

"Much appreciated," shouted Taylor as he took his seat among them.

"We're heading out in thirty minutes," replied Chandra.

"Thought we had work to finish up here?"

"We did, but Command wants to clear the path west. Those who survived and fled want their homes back, and we've got refugee camps backed up hundreds of miles. The locals are taking here, and we're moving forward to Reims ahead of schedule."

"Great, quicker the better."

"It shouldn't be long now. A few more weeks work, and the rebuilding should be able to get started."

"What then?" he asked.

"We're soldiers. We'll find a new battle to fight."

"You think they'll send us to the Moon?"

"Fucking 'ey!" yelled Silva.

"How can they not?" replied Chandra. "We have a hostile army waiting on our doorstep."

If only they could return to whatever hole they came from, thought Taylor.

"You don't seem convinced, Major? I'd have thought you of all people would want to see this through?" asked Chandra.

He nodded, but she could see he was not at all happy.

"What is it?"

He looked up at her as he chewed a mouthful of food and thought.

"I want to see an end to the war, certainly. I'd just like to see it without losing anymore friends."

The table went silent. It was the one subject all thought about and avoided discussing. Taylor looked up at their faces, realising that he wasn't being the officer they needed him to be. He felt shallow and selfish for having broken the mood.

"Ahh, don't listen to me. My head's spinning, and I didn't really sleep. I'm rambling."

"It's in all of our thoughts, but look at them," Chandra said as she pointed to the rest of the troops enjoying their meal and larking about. "They need what morale they have. Thinking what might become of us serves nobody any good."

"I know," he replied.

He already regretted voicing his bleak emotions so publically. He rubbed his weary eyes and looked up with a smile.

"I just need a coffee and all will be well," he replied.

The post war conditions had led to stagnation and a time of uncertainty. They were rebuilding while the enemy still loomed over them. They finished up as the trucks arrived to take them onwards. Chandra looked to Silva.

"Sergeant, get them loaded up."

He nodded in acknowledgement as he leaped to his

feet, bellowing his orders that echoed around the area for all to hear. Chandra got to her feet and followed Taylor so she may talk to him alone.

"You okay?" she asked.

He turned and smiled but winced as it hurt his bruised face.

"Just a rough night, is all."

"I can't tell whether it's peace you want or more war," she replied.

"Either would be better than this, just to know where we stood."

She nodded in agreement as they strode to the lead vehicle. Taylor approached to see that Eli stood there, ushering the troops aboard. She smiled at seeing him, and it was a welcome sight after the grim manner he'd previously been in. They climbed aboard and were on the move within minutes. It was a tedious journey to get out of the town as the drivers fought through the traffic and chaos, but they soon hit the open road. They were once again travelling in open country that showed no sign of the war that had passed it by. Farmhouses were deserted, and the trails of tracked vehicles through many of the fields were the only sign of the recent conflict. The snow was already beginning to cover over such sights.

"What's our job in Reims?" asked Taylor.

"Same as usual. We are to clear all roads and repair where necessary."

"Engineers work," he replied.

"Sure, but there are too few of them to work alone, and these Reitech suits surely make light work of the job. Plenty of civilians have already managed to get back, but many of the access roads are still a mess. We'll be working to the west and the road to Paris. Even the name of the city conjured up a wealth of images they all wanted to forget.

It was noon when they finally arrived in the city. Few soldiers were to be seen amongst the ruins. Many of the allied armies had quickly returned to their native lands after the enemy's retreat. Much of the city lay in ruins, and few had managed to get anywhere near the centre. A single policeman ushered their vehicles down a rubble-strewn road until they could go no further.

Taylor and Chandra leapt out from the trucks to survey the scene and gasped at the sight before them.

"Shit, this isn't going to be a quick job," shouted Taylor.

Two tower blocks had collapsed into the road in front them, and the rubble more than ten storeys high.

"We're gonna need help, lots of it," replied Chandra.

The policeman strode up beside them and patted them on the back.

"Good to have you here."

Chandra turned to him.

"We're happy to help, but we can't do it alone. We've got engineers and a few vehicles on their way to assist, but more than anything, we need manpower."

"What do you suggest I do?" he replied.

"The people returning from the east, they want their homes back, do they not?"

The man nodded.

"Then I suggest you send them our way to lend a hand. We need the roads cleared and access and communication links restored."

"I'll do what I can."

"Not good enough. I want all physically able men and women between sixteen and sixty that arrive at this city to report immediately to work detail here," growled Chandra.

The policeman looked uncomfortable and shied away, but she paced forward and grabbed the sleeve of his jacket.

"Look, this work has to get done. I don't want to be here anymore than the rest of my troops. This isn't my country. We've fought and bled over these lands so that these people could return. Show some God damn back bone and get them to lend a hand."

The man looked past the Major to the rest of the troops who stood beside the trucks silently watching him. He could see the distain in their faces.

"You will get no pity from us. We have been here from the day this war started and are still working. Get to it!" she shouted.

The officer turned and stepped slowly away towards the crossroads where they had first met him. Chandra looked at Taylor with an expression of utter shock and astonishment.

"You'd think we were an occupying army by the welcome we're getting here."

"These people are broken. We know we have homes to go back to, what do they have? They've been blasted back to the stone age," replied Taylor.

Chandra sighed. "Still no excuse for slacking and bloody rudeness after all we have done for them."

Taylor stepped up close and whispered in her ear.

"Take it easy on these people. They may not have had to fight on the frontline, but they've lost everything."

"Not their lives," she snapped.

"Plenty have. We still have no idea how many millions died in these lands."

She took a deep breath as she calmed herself and took in his words of wisdom.

"When did you become the cool headed prophet?"

"When the fighting stopped. These people aren't soldiers. They aren't under your command, and they have lost all but their lives. We need their help, but the last thing they need is abuse."

She smiled. "How you have come on, Major, so where has the marine gone that would have kicked their arses into action?"

She stepped past Taylor and patted him on the shoulder as a thank you for putting things back into perspective.

The Company still stood silently awaiting her command. They looked miserable and tired, despite the fact that work had not yet started.

"This is one of the main roads to Paris. We fought and bled over that city once and have given everything we had to get it back! This wreckage stands as much as a barrier to us as an enemy army. Would you stand here and let it tower over us in defiance? Leaving this country to ruin is to accept defeat. Every street we clear, and every town that is re-inhabited, is a victory over our enemy!"

She could hear footsteps grow nearer and turned to see a dozen men and women stroll up to her, throwing down their luggage at the side of the road. They looked up at the huge job before them and stood proud and ready. She nodded in gratitude and turned back to the troops.

"This barrier mocks us all and all the friends we have lost, let's tear it down!"

A few cheers rang out, but they were far from enthusiastic as they stepped up to the rubble and began their work. The Reitech suits provided an immense boost in strength and stamina for such labour, but it was still gruelling and mind numbing work. The troops slogged for hours, long after the civilians had lain down to rest. Finally, as the sun began to lower in the sky and cast long shadows, and the temperatures began to plummet, Chandra called them all to a halt.

She and Taylor peered around to see the results of their

work. They had cut a noticeable path to the west, but the mound of rubble appeared to have altered little.

"We need some heavy gear in here, diggers and trucks. All this crap has to go somewhere," stated Taylor.

"I am promised that the engineers are on their way, and that we will have everything we need."

They took up refuge in the nearby empty buildings for the night, alongside the growing number of civilians who were arriving to assist them. There was no alcohol that night. No parties and brawls. They were all growing tired of such activities and appreciated a quiet night of rest.

In the morning, Taylor and Chandra climbed to the top of one of the nearest intact buildings, along with several others of the Company who chose to join them. It was a vantage point no one had seen since the war had ended. There were few aerial craft available to them and just as few tall structures still standing and stable to get a viewpoint.

"My God, can this even be called a city any longer?" asked Eli.

"Makes you wonder if they'd be better off leaving this place be and build afresh."

"No, we rebuild, like humanity always has done after such times," replied Chandra.

She looked out past the vast debris they had been clearing and sighed as she squinted to see where it ended.

"We could be months clearing this," spat Taylor.

"Not once we've got the gear we need," she replied.

"I want you to take a look ahead wherever this road continues. We're getting more help all the time, and we'll soon be stepping on each other's toes. See if you can find a way through. If we can get teams to the other side and perhaps air lift a few vehicles over there, with the right help, we could halve the time this'll take."

Taylor turned back to Eli.

"Sergeant, I want you and three volunteers ready to move in ten."

She acknowledged and quickly rushed off to assemble the others down at the ground. He turned back to Chandra as she placed a hand on his shoulder.

"And be careful. We've got unstable structures, maybe unexploded ordnance, as well as the potential for remaining enemy forces, looters and all sorts. Don't forget Amiens."

He sighed as he thought back to the betrayal that still remained as a bitter experience that caused a bitter hatred of the civilian population; it would not soon be forgotten.

"I've got it, we'll find a way through. How long till you can get that air support?"

"I'm still working on it, but by the end of the day or morning at the latest."

"Great, nice of them to rush."

"This isn't a unique scene. Most of the French towns and cities that were fought over are reduced to rubble. We'll be slogging through them for months."

She went silent as they both looked out once more at

the desolate and apocalyptic looking landscape.

"Enough, we have work to do. Remember to keep in radio contact."

Taylor smiled.

"Yeah, nice to have that back. I'd almost forgotten what it was like to have personal radios."

"Our equipment developers must find a way to get around that jamming for when this war continues. For now, let's just be thankful to have it all back."

They turned and left the rooftop, taking just a last glance at the shocking sight as they trooped down towards the mountain of work which lay before them. Chandra was pleased to see that the rest of the Company and the civilians who had joined them had already begun work. They were running rubble out of the area in the troop transports that had taken them there.

"Count yourself lucky, Major. You go exploring while we slave on."

Taylor smiled, and she couldn't have been more accurate. He was aching to get ahead onto something more interesting. The fact that what waited for them the other side was the same work was something he tried to ignore and forget. He turned to see that Parker was waiting with three marines at a side alley that was still in tact.

"Alright, let's get moving."

He paced forwards to lead them and looked back just once to see Chandra step forward and get stuck in with the manual labour they had been reduced to.

"You know where this leads, Sergeant?" he asked.

"I've got maps of the area, but they are only part of the puzzle. This should be a good start for us."

"We could just use our boosters and go across the rooftops," shouted Williams.

Taylor nodded and sighed at the same time.

"It's appealing certainly, but if only we can make it, that doesn't help."

"If we just had some damn birds in the air, we could sort this problem in no time," replied Clark.

Taylor stopped and turned back to them with a stern face.

"We're using old tech and tactics, I get it. Look around you. Maybe last year we had access to whatever we wanted and needed, but that just ain't the case anymore. It's not exactly glamorous work, but at least nobody is shooting at us. Now, can we carry on with a little less bitching?"

A large aircraft burst across the sky, sending vibrations through the ground. For a moment they all flinched. They had become accustomed to expecting anything above them to be enemy craft. They relaxed as they saw a friendly transport plane rush over the city at remarkably low altitude. Taylor relaxed and righted himself. As he began to speak, Lam leapt forward and pushed him aside, and the others scattered. A chunk of concrete almost the size of a car crashed down between them.

Taylor pushed Lam off him and looked around with a panic to see if Parker was okay. They had all scattered with just a metre or two between them, and a crushing and immediate death. He patted Lam on the shoulder.

"Thanks," he snarled.

"Bloody flyboys!" yelled Parker.

Taylor tapped his intercom. "Chandra, this is Taylor, over."

"Already on it, Major. We have a few light injuries here, but everyone is okay. What is your status, over?"

"Near miss, but we're all okay, over."

"Time for someone to get a grilling. Good luck, over and out."

Taylor turned back to the other four marines who looked distinctly unimpressed.

"Fucking idiots," snapped Lam.

"As if it wasn't enough that we had an advanced alien race trying to make us extinct, our own bloody people are trying to kill us," replied Taylor.

"I'm sure they were on an urgent mission to bring General Schulz his afternoon snack," Parker grinned.

"Alright, let's get moving."

They wandered for hours through side streets and derelict buildings, trying to find a safe route through, and marking their waypoints as they went.

"Can't we just use the city ring road?" asked Lam.

"No, it's bumper to bumper with abandoned cars, and

a hell of a way to have to walk it. The civilians who fled in a panic clogged the roads solid and had to leave on foot. First thing we have to do is establish a straight route through towards Paris."

They continued on through the blown windows of a shop front and into another alleyway. They reached a mound of bricks that had collapsed in from a small explosion. Mitch lifted his Mappad and studied it carefully.

"Access here could open up the route we need. It may be worth clearing."

He noticed a roof access ladder that was still intact just a few metres back.

"Make a start on it. I'll head to the roof and see what the situation is up ahead, make sure it's worth our time."

He strode over and placed his hands on the bars of the ladder.

"You know you could jump it," muttered Eli.

"True, but call me old fashioned, I like to do some of the work myself."

He began to climb the ladder and felt less than his body weight as the suit propelled him quickly to the roof. As he neared the top, he felt one of the rusted metal steps buckle under the weight of him and all his gear. He took a firm grasp with his hands on the rungs and hoisted himself up without incident. Mitch looked down from the roof to see he had climbed eight storeys while the others had only just begun to start working.

The cool icy wind hit his face from the exposed rooftop. Many of the structures around the building were at least partially still standing, but he could see several collapsed skyscrapers dotted across the city. He looked down again to the rubble blocking their path. He nodded as he realised that they could clear the way with an hour's labour.

Morbid curiosity overcame the Major, and he turned and strolled across the rooftop, looking out across the rest of the devastation. Just as he reached the centre of the roof, he felt the floor under his feet shake. Before he could respond, it gave way beneath him. Taylor collapsed through a gaping hole that he had created and quickly crashed into the next floor down. The weight and bulk of his body and equipment made him to smash through the floor.

Black ash and dust filled his throat and chest as he continued to descend through floor after floor. The entire internals of the structure had been destroyed by fire. The weak floors were providing just enough cushioning to slow his fall but enough to hurt like hell.

Finally, after he broke through the fourth floor, he landed hard on a solid surface, and the wind was taken out of him. His back plate took the worst of the impact, but it jolted his body. His ass went numb from the landing, and his helmet lashed against the ground, stunning him for a moment. He shook his head to clear the dust, but it only served to clog his windpipe further as a soot cloud arose around him.

As he regained his composure, he could hear the faint sounds of his comrades shouting and calling for him. He tapped his intercom, but it did nothing. The impact had destroyed it. He reached for his rifle that had been slung on his back, only to realise it was long gone. He looked up through the breach he had created and saw the smashed weapon hung by its broken sling on the sixth floor.

"Shit," he muttered.

Taylor sat up and tried to wipe his eyes with his hands, but they were just as dirty as his face. His gear was so coated in the black soot that he blended in with almost perfect camouflage to the ruined structure. He looked around at his surroundings, but there was little to see but more debris and black walls in what used to be an office compound.

A faint mechanical sound rang out to his other side, and Taylor snapped his head around just in time to see the wall cave in just ten metres away. His heart stopped as he recognised the towering height of what was coming through the breach when part of the floor above collapsed between them. A single Mech was visible through the falling dust.

"Shit," he whispered.

Taylor rolled over several times to his side until he came up against a desk that hid him from the creature's view.

Where the fuck did that come from?

He reached down for the pistol he always carried, but it was nowhere to be found; another item lost during his fall. His eyes grew wide at the realisation that he was in real trouble.

Looking down, he could see that all he had on him was a single frag grenade and his Assegai. He took a deep breath and held it as he listened intently all round him. The creature stepped slowly around and had clearly not discovered his position yet. He peered out over the top of a workstation just enough to get a glance of what he faced. The creature was almost as filthy as him. Its armour had been damaged through fighting, but not enough to impede its ability.

He could still hear the cries of his comrades outside, and he prayed they would stop. Just as he thought it, they did. *Please no*, he thought. He hoped they were onto the situation rather than silenced by any of the creature's allies. He could hear the steps of the huge creature growing nearer and knew he was running out of time and space. He slowly crawled along the table edge until he could turn a corner and be out of sight. Taylor could hear that he had turned the bend just a few seconds before he would have been found.

He took a deep breath and tried to calm himself, realising he had no choice but to take on the beast in close combat. They were too close for the grenade to be used without a serious risk of hurting himself. The explosion would be more than capable of tearing through most of the room. His sweaty hand reached for the hilt of his Assegai, and he slowly drew it from its sheath.

The heavy steps of the creature stomped closer; almost in tune with his heart that was now calm. He had accepted what he must do, and the fear was draining away. His back was against an office divider, and he was down on one knee. His head was turned awaiting the sight of the beast. The barrel of its huge weapon came around the corner first, and he knew it was his opportunity to strike.

Taylor leapt up and thrust his Assegai forwards. The creature tried to turn its hulking weapon around, but the Assegai punctured into the main body of the cannon. The alien responded by striking him to the chest with a forceful push, launching him two metres back and onto the top of a desk.

He looked up just in time to see the cannon being trained on him. The creature pulled the trigger, but the weapon did nothing. He smiled in relief; his strike had disabled the fearful thing. The angry creature threw it down and rushed towards him. The hulking beast was twice his bulk, and like a rhino bearing down on him. He rolled off the table just in time as it crushed it before him.

Taylor ducked under a swing from the creature and thrust up against the clumsy Mech into its rib area. It spasmed in pain as the Assegai was forced in all the way to its hilt. He tore it out as thick blue blood spewed out from the punctured armour. He could see the energy fade in the beast, and it dropped down on one leg. He spun the Assegai around, and took it in both hands above his head with the dripping tip pointing to the ground.

The beast tried with all its energy to reach for him, but he thrust down into its faceplate with all his force. The cutting torch style tip needed little pressure to penetrate the thick armour, but it made Taylor feel better to release his anger. The beast went immediately limp and slumped backwards. He wrenched the Assegai from the corpse, and thick blood clung to the entire length of the blade.

"Fucking disgusting," he exclaimed as he spat on the body of his vanquished foe. He stood and peered at the lifeless hulk with some satisfaction. Weeks of slogging labour had made him forget how much he enjoyed killing. A thunderous drone rang out from an adjoining room, and he turned just in time to see the thin wall smashed through by three armed aliens. They trained their weapons on him before he had a moment to react. He stood tall and stared them down, for he did not want to die cowered down in a hole.

"Alien scum," he spat.

A massive explosion erupted before him and at the feet of the creatures, and the Mechs collapsed through a vast hole. Dust and debris showered Taylor. He turned away as the smoke once again filled his lungs. He looked in surprise at the breach as gunfire erupted in the floor below. Automatic weapon fire from his comrades tore the creatures apart.

The Major paced forward and looked down through the gaping hole, just in time to see the last rounds puncture the aliens' armour and render them lifeless. He watched as Eli stepped up and laid a boot on a beast's body before firing a final round through its faceplate. She looked up and smiled as she made out the dusty silhouette of Taylor.

"Thought we'd lost you there for a minute!"

"Outstanding," he replied.

Taylor leapt through the breach and used just a fraction of boost to soften his landing.

"Let's get the hell out of this shithole."

"I figure we've blown our way in this far, we might as well use this to work round that blocked alley."

"Lead the way, Sergeant," he replied.

Ten minutes later they were huddled behind a solid foundation wall.

"Fire in the hole!" Parker shouted.

She lifted an arming device and punched down the trigger. A small explosion rang out, and they turned to see that a two metre wide hole had been punched through the outer wall and out into an open shopping street.

"We're in business," said Taylor.

They strode out into the daylight. At the far end of the road, they could see the rubble pile blocking the main street that Chandra was trying to clear.

"Alright, we've done it. Send the route back to Major Chandra. How long do you figure it'll take to walk the distance?" he asked.

"I figure about twenty-five minutes, now we've got a clear route."

Parker stopped and looked at Taylor and the state he was in. The thick black soot and dust clung to every part of his body and equipment. She suddenly burst into laughter at the sight of him. He looked down at the mess, thought back to the near death experience, and could do nothing but laugh as well.

"You lot saved my ass back there. Another second, and I was a goner."

"Nothing you haven't done for us, Major," replied Lam.

"We were wrong to think this was over. The enemy didn't surrender, and they didn't sign any treaty. We've been walking around as if they were gone for good," mused Eli.

Taylor lifted up his hands, looking at the congealed blue blood staining them and running down the metal forearm bars of his exoskeleton. He had lost the stomach for war so quickly, but in just one small action, he was reminded of the bloodlust they had all built in the war.

"Guess we need to find you a weapon, Sir," said Clark.

The Major looked down at his hands once again and suddenly felt naked at the realisation that he was without a gun.

"Reiter won't be happy you lost his toys," joked Parker.

"We came way too close today. We're trying to rebuild this country before we've even finished fighting."

He lifted his hand to activate his comms unit, and then remembered it had been destroyed on impact.

"Get Chandra back on the line. It's time we took this seriously and got some troops up ahead of the work. I want these lands purged of the infection of these Krycenaean bastards!"

CHAPTER THREE

Taylor had arrived back at their staging ground for just a few seconds when a jeep roared into view as if an urgent message was to be delivered. It was a sight they had gotten used to under the enemy jamming systems. He paced up beside Chandra who had also turned to find the meaning of such urgency.

"What do you think they need us for now? Another heap of shit I'm sure," whispered Taylor.

She turned and looked at the filthy Major. "You met some resistance, I hear?"

Taylor turned with a puzzled expression. "You don't seem surprised?"

"It was bound to happen soon enough. The real question is were those Mechs stranded here, or were they stationed here?"

The jeep slid to a halt, and the driver leapt out to

address them.

"I guess we're about to find out," replied Taylor.

The German Sergeant quickly saluted and immediately blurted out his message.

"Ma'am, your presence is urgently requested."

"By whom?" she calmly responded.

"General Schulz. He wants Major Taylor also."

Taylor's eyes widened at the prospect. He couldn't imagine any reason why Schulz would want to see him, other than incarcerating him once more. Schulz had tried to ease the conflict between them, but Taylor firmly believed it was only to ensure the morale of the troops stayed high.

She nodded in agreement and turned to Captain Jones.

"Get a party together to start work the other side of this blockade, but I want you to personally scour the buildings. Be prepared for ambush. Take Yorath's platoon with you, but be certain to leave protection at both sites."

"You expect more trouble?" he asked.

"Most certainly. We've got lazy since we drove their forces back. Let's keep everyone safe. This country has a chance to rebuild, so let's not allow anything to get in the way of that, not least our own negligence."

She turned back to the driver. "You ready?"

The man nodded and ushered them quickly into his vehicle.

The two Majors sat in the back of the jeep as they tore

through the streets. There was little traffic going east. As the wind rushed through the open topped vehicle and they hit the open road, the two of them were able to speak without their driver listening in.

"I don't like this at all. Schulz has fucked us before, what makes you think he's honourable enough to trust?" asked Taylor.

"He isn't. He may be a bastard, but he isn't stupid. Now that the fighting is over, he'll have the whole of your Marine Corps on his arse if he dares touch you. Think what your President would have to say if he learnt that one of its greatest heroes was being arrested?"

"It didn't stop the bastard before."

"We were at war. Times have changed," she replied.

"You told me the war wasn't over."

She smiled. "True, it's merely on hold."

They arrived at a temporary air base on the eastern edge of France that had been established since the war had ended. It was a hive of activity as vehicles came and went between the multitude of fighters and transport craft lined across the strip. They pulled up beside a concrete structure that had only the letters 'HQ' upon it. Outside were military police guards who wore impeccable white webbing over their perfectly pressed uniforms.

Taylor and Chandra leapt off the vehicle under the gaze of the guards who looked at their filthy uniforms with disgust. Taylor glared back at them and could not resist a taunt.

"Those rifles look as clean as a whistle, ever fired them?"

The two men stared back, and he could see they were desperate to confront him. One of them who wore sergeant's stripes moved a single pace forward and saw the Major's rank crowns hidden beneath the black soot that still coated him. The Sergeant hesitated and stepped back into position. Taylor grinned in satisfaction.

"Enough taunting them, we've got real work to do."

She knew her comments would only infuriate the MPs further, which served to entertain Taylor.

"Please, follow me!" shouted the driver as he rushed into the HQ building.

They followed him through and into a room with a large planning table and a dozen high-ranking officers sat about it. They all wore their service dress and were belittled by the two filthy officers in their bulky armour and exoskeletons.

"How dare you step into our presence in such a state!" declared Dupont.

Taylor shot a wicked glance back at the General and stood defiantly before him.

"You'll excuse our attire, for we were informed we were to get to you with all haste. Nor do we currently possess any uniforms besides these. As combat troops, we only carry what we need," explained Chandra.

Dupont was infuriated by what she was insinuating but knew it was worded in such a way that he could do nothing in return. He spun around to address Schulz who was sat calmly at the head of the table.

"Will you suffer these filthy soldiers here?" he asked.

Schulz launched his chair backwards as he shot up to his feet.

"Will you shut up!" he yelled.

Taylor smiled as he saw the shock in Dupont's face, and the man's shoulders slump as he was humiliated before them all.

That's right, you son of a bitch, thought Taylor.

Dupont went silent and lay back with a smirk. Schulz sighed as he sat back down and pulled his chair into the table. He took look around the room and took one last deep breath before he addressed them all.

"Tensions have been high. There have been some hot headed actions and enough scorn and bitterness to last a lifetime. This is war, so let us not forget that all of us here are on the same side."

He paused for a moment for his words to settle in. Taylor, for the first time since he had met the General, began to understand his position. Schulz wasn't an inherently bad person, far from it. He was a plotter and a thinker, and a man who saw the big picture; and had no time to fret over one soldier's single death. Taylor sometimes wished he could have commanded some of the battles in the war but also saw the toll it took.

"Soldiers and civilians alike are slaving every day to try and clear roads, and get this country back on its feet. Major Chandra, you are probably not aware that we have had substantial resources put into Paris. The capital is an important symbol for this world, and it must be operational as quickly as possible."

"Is there much left of it?" muttered Taylor.

Schulz heard his quiet words and stopped to address the question.

"Enough that it is, and always will be, Paris. The two of you are more than aware of what the enemy were doing with the former capital."

"Actually, Sir, we may have seen a lot, but we understood little of it."

"Exactly so. The city has been deemed safe, and what is left of the government is already being re-instated there. The leaders of many of the key armies of the world are assembling there to witness first hand the sights which you yourselves uncovered."

"To what end, Sir?" she asked.

Taylor could see that Dupont was desperate to leap to his feet and shoot them down in flames, but he held his tongue in the knowledge he would only receive a second ridiculing.

"What your reports described was deeply disturbing. Experts from around the world have been let into the site in the last few weeks, and we all hope they have some answers. I would like both of you to join us on this journey. Perhaps you can shed more light on whatever was going on there."

Taylor turned to Chandra, and she could see in his eyes that he didn't want to go. She also knew that Schulz was making a determined effort to repair the relationship with her Company, and specifically with Mitch.

"What about our unit, Sir?"

"Captain Jones will be more than capable of managing. I am sending an infantry company with a detachment of engineers to assist them. They'll be arriving this evening."

"Thank you, Sir. We'd be more than happy to accompany you to Paris, but I cannot promise that we'll be any assistance in understanding what is there."

* * *

Jones paced cautiously along a roadside, looking in every window and alcove as he passed. Abandoned cars still littered the roads. Some were burnt out wrecks, while others seemed to have past through the conflict like a time capsule. Brick dust and other grime covered every visible surface, and huge craters were still littering the streets.

"Need to get those bloody engineers here, and get these holes filled in!" Monty shouted.

Jones stopped and turned to watch his unit pass

through the rubble and debris of the city. He shook his head in astonishment. It was hard to believe that it could ever return to its former glory. He caught a glimmer of light in the distance as light reflected off a moving object. The Captain quickly lifted his binoculars.

His body went taut at the thought they were not alone. He panned around to find the source of the light, and then finally down to the street ahead could see Yorath and his unit coming out from a side alley up ahead. He let go of the binoculars and let them rest on his chest as he peered around at all the derelict structures around them. He hoped friendly forces were the source of the glimmer, but he doubted they were so lucky.

Just as he felt his shoulders relax, an explosion ripped through the street in the distance, and the ground shook beneath them. Jones instinctively leapt for cover and tumbled across the road. He ran over broken glass before landing back on one knee beside an upturned police cruiser. His heart sunk, as he already knew that yet another comrade and friend would be dead. He prayed for it not to be the case, but it was unavoidable.

Jones took a deep breath and raised himself up high enough to peer over the vehicle down towards Yorath's unit. There were no screams or sounds of gunfire. The apocalyptical street was once more silent as all of the soldiers in it froze beside their cover. They awaited the onslaught of an enemy barrage or ambush, but it never came.

"Come in Yorath, report," he whispered.

Static came over his mic and the sound of breathing as the Lieutenant tried to find the words to tell him.

"We've, we've got two down."

"What is their status?"

"One wounded, and he'll make it. The other is gone."

Jones shook his head in anger.

"We made it through. This is bullshit," whispered Jones to himself.

He looked up and all around for some signs of the enemy, but he already speculated that it was a planted explosive of some sort.

"Any indication of enemies in the vicinity?" he asked.

"None."

Jones stood up from behind the car and walked casually towards Yorath's platoon. Jones' unit followed after him, though more cautiously. They reached the scene of the explosion and could see Private Nichols had been torn apart by the blast and killed instantly.

At least there's enough left for a funeral. It's more than most have got these last months, thought Jones.

A few metres away, the medic was attending to the other casualty. Jones could see the wounds were only superficial from shrapnel. The man's body armour showed deep scrapes and scars where the cuirass had saved his life. He was more stunned that hurt.

"Shit, this isn't how it's supposed to have gone," whispered Jones.

He spoke under his breath so that others wouldn't hear, but he did not have such luck. Yorath got to his feet and stepped up beside the Captain.

"What are we even still doing here? Haven't we given enough for this country? We should go home, and let their own people sort this mess out. I didn't see civilians rushing forward to help fight this war, so why should we do all the work?" he asked.

Jones winced at the fact the Lieutenant had made his despondent words loud enough for many around them to hear. Charlie leaned in close and whispered to Yorath.

"I'll remind you that you are an officer in the British Army, not some loud mouthed thug. Look at them, all of them. Their morale is low enough as it is. Last thing they need is an officer inciting insubordination in their ranks. We'll leave when we're ordered to."

"And when will that be?" snapped Yorath. "When there aren't enough of us left to be what is deemed effective?"

"Don't give me this shit. You think doing a little hard labour is tough? Try being a prisoner of those bastards!"

Yorath went quiet. He was shamed into silence by the Captain, who he knew in his heart he should support and respect.

Jones turned and walked over to the wounded man and knelt down beside him.

"You'll be just fine."

The man nodded in gratitude, staring at the body of his friend who had not been so lucky.

"We won't be able to get vehicles out here for a while, and it seems any assistance in the air is too much to ask right now. My platoon will continue to scour the area for enemy combatants and devices. Yorath, you will return to base with the wounded and take some rest."

The Lieutenant smiled at the sympathy Jones was showing them, but he could not feel any better about their situation. Rest was all very well, but they would only have to return to the same wastelands afterwards. Jones stood up and stepped towards the blast area. He stood for a moment carefully studying it.

"Look at the damage, and remember what it sounded like. That wasn't an enemy weapon. There must be unexploded ordnance in the area. Nichols must have triggered it somehow."

"Great, blown up by our own bombs," replied Monty.

"You remember the battle we fought in this city. Half the time we couldn't tell where the lines were anymore and fire was coming in all over. This won't be the last time we get bitten by our own bombs."

"They need to get teams over here to deal with this shit," growled Blinker.

"Half the country is this way, so they're gonna be spread thin. For now we must tread a little lighter. Be alert. Just because this was one of ours, it doesn't mean the enemy haven't planted mines and other devices."

Jones stood and watched with sadness as the body of Nichols was whisked away, and Yorath's platoon trundled wearily back to the work site that in that moment was their home.

"I can't believe he made it all the way through this war only to be killed now. I saw him take a pulse to the chest and keep fighting in Ramstein. Poor bastard," Blinker continued.

Jones lifted his weapon and gave it a quick check before turning to his unit. He could see in their faces they were tired of it all. They didn't want to continue on their days to meet the same fate as Nichols. He did not blame them. He wanted revenge against the invaders, but it was the one thing they could not get.

"Major Taylor nearly lost his life because these buildings weren't cleared. What happens when a family comes home to discover one of the creatures among them? They'll get torn apart. We won this victory, let's see it through!" yelled Jones.

It was hard to motivate fatigued veteran soldiers to continue in both a menial and dangerous task. He continually questioned their duty and responsibility to the country himself, but he was a stickler for orders.

"We've got work to do, let's move out!"

* * *

Taylor peered out of the window as their craft banked to encircle the centre of Paris. There was no need to still be in the air for any reason but to gain an aerial view of the devastation and work that went on below. Many of the high-ranking officers around them gasped at the sight below. Taylor had no physical response at all.

Inside, he felt pain soar through his body. The sight of the obliterated city was a constant reminder of old wounds, injuries that had for all intensive purposes had time to recover.

"I never thought we'd make it to this day," whispered Chandra.

"To see a beautiful city in ruin?" replied Taylor.

"No, to see it reborn. Only a few months ago we couldn't bring a halt to their advances, and now look where we are."

"With a bunch of desk jockey assholes going to revel in their glorious victory."

Chandra smiled. Dupont had been listening in from the row behind them, but they hadn't noticed his presence. The General's face was of hate and scorn, but he dared not take the fight to Taylor at that time. He plotted and schemed while better men and women fought and died.

From the window, it was clear that resources had been poured into Paris. They could see thousands of construction vehicles at work. Two cranes were already put to work on the Eiffel Tower, rebuilding the iconic symbol of France.

"So this is why we aren't getting any help."

As he said the words, they saw two large transport craft land in the centre of the city.

"Paris was a bastion of hope for us all. To rebuild it is the ultimate act of defiance to the enemy."

"I thought that was going to the Moon and kicking their asses?"

"All in good time."

A few minutes later, their craft put down on a landing zone with the wing of fighters that were attached as a protection detail. As they stepped out onto the tarmac, they were greeted by a host of officers and politicians in all manner of uniforms and insignia. The French President and Prime Minister were at the centre of the party which Schulz and Dupont headed to.

"Major Taylor."

Mitch turned at the stern manner in which is name was called. General White stood to his flank with several other US officers. A broad smile stretched across his face as he looked down at Taylor's scruffy uniform that had only received the quickest of brush downs.

"Your presentation seems to have gone rather downhill since coming this side of the pond," he jested.

Taylor reached out and shook White's hand.

"Damn good to see you again, Sir."

"I have to say you were sorely missed during the last few months."

"You seemed to manage just fine, Sir."

"Please follow this way!" called Schulz.

The General led the French leaders towards the monstrous enemy structures which Taylor and Chandra were all too familiar with.

"So this is where you killed the bastard?" asked White.

"Not alone, Sir. The Company under the command of Major Chandra here excelled themselves."

White shook her hand and nodded in gratitude.

"I believe we have met in previous years."

"Yes, Sir."

"Taylor under your command? Times have changed!"

They were led to the site where they had previously seen humans incubated for as far as the eye could see. As they stepped from the corridor out into the vast hall, they gasped at the sight of the equipment once again. The humans, or what appeared to be humans, had long gone, but the chambers remained. Schulz stopped the column and addressed them before the alien technology.

"From the reports of Major Chandra and her Company, we know that these chambers were occupied up until the enemy retreat. Our best experts so far believe that the humans within them were being used either as some power or food source, or potentially for experimental purposes.

We certainly know that they were keen to establish creative ways to end our race."

Chandra looked down at the bulkheads and walls that still bore the scorch marks from their battle. It still didn't feel real that they had won.

"How did we ever do it?" she asked Taylor.

"What?"

"Win. In the opening months of the war, we faced extinction. How did we ever turn it around?"

"We aren't the only soldiers to have turned the tide in great battles and wars."

"If it had been you that had landed here on foreign soil and been forced out with such losses, would you let it go? Would you return to your home world and forget?"

Taylor contemplated the question for a moment before realizing that he only had one answer.

"I'd want payback."

"Even as the aggressor?"

"Sure. Only a coward would turn tail and run."

She nodded in agreement. "Then this war isn't over. Maybe it can never be over."

Schulz's voice echoed around the hall as he led on the party through the enemy facility. Taylor and Chandra remained silent as they both pondered her realization. Then Mitch looked up and his eyes grew wider and mouth drier as he recognized where they were heading.

"This is where we took down Karadag."

"You know I have been dying to see this spot," muttered White. "Where mere humans killed a titan."

The General patted Mitch on the back.

"He was a formidable opponent. I never thought I'd see the day when a war could be decided in single combat."

"It wasn't, Sir. Sergeant Parker was by my side. No one soldier could have beaten that bastard. I can still barely believe that we managed it."

"You did your country and the world the greatest service here. No one should forget that. You will be honoured appropriately in time."

"Honoured?"

The General looked puzzled.

"The only honour I would ask is to go home, or somewhere I could call home."

White smiled but was also surprised at his words. The group came to a standstill as Schulz turned and stood triumphantly at the place where Karadag fell. His blood still stained the metal floor, but his body was long gone; whisked away by the enemy as they fled from the planet.

"This is where it all happened, where the creature known as Karadag met his end at the hands of the 2nd Inter-Allied under the command of these two fine officers!" shouted Schulz as he beckoned towards the two of them.

Cheers and fierce clapping rang out as all attention was on Chandra and Taylor. Mitch noticed neither of them was mentioned by name, but he didn't let it bother him. As far as he was concerned, the victory belonged to all who contributed to the war effort. Attention soon focused on the German General, and White turned back to Taylor.

"I hear they're still keeping you busy here, Major."

"Clean up work," he replied.

"And a little more than that. You nearly got yourself killed earlier today," Chandra added.

"Go on," continued White.

"Found a few stragglers in Reims, nothing we couldn't handle."

"Yes, I have been hearing more about pockets of enemy forces. There is chatter about assembling a few hunting teams to sort them out. Your names have been floating about as you're more than suited to the task."

Taylor's eyes lit up. He was all for helping the civilian population, but their lives had ground to a monotonous halt. The near death experience earlier now felt like a spark of excitement in their tedious lives.

"Sounds like our kind of work."

"Good. Now, those cells, or chambers we saw just now. What the hell do you propose they were doing there?"

Taylor sighed at the thought of it as Chandra stepped in.

"We've thought and talked it over almost every day since, Sir, but it's only speculation."

"Well, go on then, speculate."

"I believe they were being readied as an army against

us. I wouldn't like to say if they were captured humans, or some kind of cloned or genetically created beings. It's clear we have given the enemy a much harder fight that they could have imagined."

White nodded in agreement. He wasn't shocked at all by the theory as she continued on.

"We outnumbered them in every major engagement, and once we had started to modify their own technology, they were overwhelmed. Despite everything we had developed, they were still better soldier for soldier. What they needed more than anything was manpower."

"Based on the number of incubation chambers, if they had gotten those people into combat, the war could have gone very differently," whispered White. "I won't lie to you, we were having a rough time of it back home. Germany would have quickly fallen, and the joint armies that fought across France and over the Rhine would have been encircled within weeks. It's a damn miracle what you pulled off."

"How many of those incubation cells are there?" Taylor asked.

"From what I understand, five hundred thousand or more. That's a lot of manpower."

"We need to know what they were planning," mused Taylor.

"Can't we just be happy we won?" asked Chandra.

"To lower our guard so soon after a narrow victory

would be foolish indeed," replied White.

The next hour was filled with questions for the two Majors that neither could answer. They were quizzed as if they were intelligence officers, when all they did was fight. After an exhausting grilling by the Command staff, they were finally allowed to leave aboard another plane. The two of them slumped into the comfortable seats of a luxury civilian transport, sighing in relief as they finally laid to rest.

The plane could seat fifty, but only five were aboard. Few would choose to leave the recovering capitol for the ruins of Reims.

"What was the point of it all?" asked Taylor.

"We've got to do our best to understand our enemy," she replied.

"I understand that, but they have experts for that. Our job is to fight."

"Schulz wanted to revel in his victory. Word is spreading of your defeat of Karadag, but many still do not believe it. There's no body as proof, no video footage, just the word of one gung ho marine who is hated by Command, and claims to have slain a monster with only the aid and confirmation of his girlfriend. Would you believe it?"

Taylor smiled.

"You should have been there. I still can't believe we managed it."

The two went silent as the craft lifted off and headed

back to the only home they knew.

"You heard White. Taskforces are being created to hunt down the remaining forces, and we're right at the top of the list."

"Because of our reputation, or because certain individuals are still hoping they can get me killed before this is over?"

"Both I should think. The Company is restless. They need something to occupy their minds. We aren't talking about a meat grinder here. Hunting a handful of Mechs with the numbers and firepower we have should be exactly what we need."

"Agreed."

"Captain Jones."

"What of him?"

"I wasn't there when you all took on Karadag as you have just mentioned, and your report did not reflect it, but I know Jones went wild. He has had a death wish. Do you believe he is over it?"

"Back then I would have said no, but you saw him with Dubois. He's a changed man, and back to his old self."

"You believe it could all change overnight?"

"You'd be amazed what the love of a good woman can do."

"I'll take your word for it. I agree, though. I thought we'd lost him for good. On that note, we'll be getting our orders regarding this new matter tomorrow, and I'm sure that Command will be keen to get us in the field ASAP. I've seen enough drunken exploits to last a lifetime. Take it easy tonight, and rest up for the morning."

Taylor trundled back to his billet. He felt like a week had been crammed into the day, and he was once again left in the lurch, awaiting some news of what they were to do. He opened the door on the popup shelter to find Eli comfortably asleep inside. It wasn't quite the coming home to his own house experience but was an appealing sight, nonetheless.

As he pulled off his equipment and clothing, she rolled over and slowly came to. A smile came over her face as she watched him take his shirt off and reveal his toned but scarred body.

"Hey, stranger," she whispered.

"I thought you'd be out having a drink."

"I figured we've done enough damage," she laughed.

He sat down on the edge of the bed as she got up to hold him. She ran her hands softly over his body. His arms and legs were bruised and scraped from his fall, and he winced in pain as he found so many muscles and bones to be throbbing.

"How much more of this do you think you can survive?" she asked.

"I'm still standing, aren't I?"

"Just about."

He turned to see if she was truly worried for him

but quickly realized she was merely having fun. His own mortality was always something that prayed on his mind.

"How are we still alive?" he asked. "All the crazy shit we've done, and made it through?"

"Our training, skills, common sense, and a heap load of luck."

Taylor sighed. "That's reassuring."

He lay down and took a deep breath as he settled in comfortably beneath the sheets, and Eli huddled up next to him.

"You almost died today," she whispered. "Remember the rules, never go anywhere alone. Just because the enemy is in retreat, doesn't mean it's over. None of us are safe."

He nodded in agreement. He kicked himself for being so reckless, but without such a visible enemy to fight, it was hard not to try and move on from it all. He felt an immense feeling of satisfaction rush through his body that almost made him shiver.

All the drinking and partying we have done, and this feels a whole world better.

Taylor drifted into a calm and tranquil sleep as if he'd been waiting for it for months.

CHAPTER FOUR

Taylor awoke early and feeling fresh, unlike the previous few weeks when his head throbbed. He was up and out of bed in a flash. His ripped and filthy uniform from the day before was gone, and a fresh pristine replacement lay in its place. Parker was already gone, and he could only assume she was responsible for the service.

As he pulled on his clothing, he could hear Silva shouting outside, calling the Company to attention. He rushed to the door as he buttoned his shirt just in time to see a jeep pull up with Commander Phillips on board. The road they had set up in was largely covered by a huge shelter that span the full width to the buildings either side. Mess tables filled the shelter, but a roadway had been maintained through the centre where the officer's vehicle arrived.

Phillips leapt from the vehicle with a smile as he

approached Chandra. Taylor quickly hopped to her side and seemed to be the last soldier to awake.

"Didn't think we'd be seeing you anytime soon, Sir," she pondered.

"No, but Command has a new job for your Company, and they have placed me in command of this part of the operation."

"Search and destroy?" asked Taylor.

Phillips nodded with a surprised expression.

"We were in for quite a surprise yesterday, Sir. It's clear there is still some fighting to be done here."

"Well, it's nice to hear you're up to speed, Major," he snapped.

Taylor could see it bothered the Commander that he clearly already knew their orders before they had been relayed. He had passed on General White's news to Chandra as well, but she saw fit not to put the Commander out of place by saying so. A few minutes later, they were sat at one of the tables, discussing the planned operations as trucks continued to roll through the huge shelter and carrying debris away.

"There have been a number of incidents in previously occupied territories, unfortunate encounters. Some have involved allied troops and been dealt with to varying degrees of success. However, other situations have occurred where civilians have stumbled upon the enemy and no mercy has been shown. The last thing we need is the civilian population living in fear of the monsters hiding in their own backyard."

"Have there been many fatalities?" asked Chandra.

"A few. Media links are still poor, and that's saved it from becoming a widespread epidemic. However, that situation can't last forever. We need these pockets of resistance cleared quickly."

"How many are we talking?" asked Taylor.

"Quite honestly, we have no idea. We don't know if these are enemy soldiers who got left behind during their hasty retreat, or if they were planted specifically. All we know is it is seriously hindering our efforts. Clean up crews have to be protected at all times, and that is a logistical nightmare. We've also lost a number of soldiers because of these encounters."

"And we're expected to do this all alone?" asked Chandra.

"No, a taskforce is being assembled in each country. Mostly they'll be taken from native forces, but the French military is weak and spread thin. Your Company has a thorough grasp of warfare in this land and is more than up to the task."

"We gonna get the resources we need?" asked Taylor.

"I have been given the authority to provide any and all assistance required."

Taylor smiled in surprise. "Wow, looks like we really are getting out of this shithole."

"Out of the frying pan and all that," whispered Chandra.

"What is the strength of this Company?" asked Phillips.

"One hundred and twenty three," she replied.

"Far from full strength, but more than suitable for this new task."

They stopped as two of the Company delivered mugs of tea and coffee to them. The heater modules kept them all from freezing, but a hot drink was always welcome when you looked out at the weather conditions which were rapidly worsening.

"We'll need transport and more than a few jeeps," stated Taylor.

"Already en route. General White has attached three copters to you for the duration of this taskforce. Lieutenant Rains and his comrades are en route as we speak. They'll be putting down in the Parc de Champagne shortly. It's just south of here and will become your staging ground for now."

"What about this place?"

"A Gendarmerie detachment will be arriving within the hour to relieve you. Chandra, I want you to assemble the Company and move out. You'll have to make your way to the Parc on foot, but once you're there, you'll have everything you need."

Forty-five minutes later they were once again traipsing through the war torn streets, but this time with a newfound enthusiasm. They reached the Parc by noon to find the three copters had already arrived, along with several support craft and transports. Marines guarded the perimeter of the site and made it most welcoming. The corporal on the main entrance through a stone wall saluted as they approached.

"As you were!" shouted Chandra.

"Ma'am, it's an honour to work alongside the Immortals."

She shrugged at the name. It never sat comfortably with her after seeing the deaths of so many friends. She nodded as a greeting and continued past the man towards where Eddie was sat with his feet up and a cup of coffee. He looked more relaxed than ever as he lifted his mug, and a huge smile expanded across his face when he saw the two Majors approaching.

"Still alive and kicking!" he yelled.

"Same to you, how you been?" asked Taylor.

"Ah, you know, got my feathers burnt a few times, but I'm alive to tell the tale. Word is we're on hunting duty, that right?"

"You got it," replied Taylor.

"Command gives us intel. We respond immediately with a ground assault, supported by artillery and/or air support where needed," Chandra added.

"There may Mechs left in this neck of the woods?"

"Enough," replied Taylor.

Chandra felt the vibration of a message being received

on her Mappad. She pulled it from her webbing. The two men watched and waiting impatiently for news until she looked up at them in surprise.

"This is it, our first co-ordinates."

"Christ, they aren't hanging around."

"We can rest our feet on the boats," she replied and turned to Eddie.

"You lot ready to roll?"

"Yes, Ma'am," he replied with a smile.

"Then get moving, we're wheels up in five."

She turned back to the Company who were stood as a mass, awaiting their orders. More than anything they looked bored.

"Our first operation has been green lit, we move in five!"

A cheer rang out from the troops, but she quickly lifted up her palm to signal for silence.

"Section and Platoon leaders to me. The rest of you, mount up!"

The NCOs and officers gathered beside the supply dump as the troops stomped past into the copters.

"Our first target is in the town of Troyes, a little over a hundred clicks from here. A short journey now we've got wings. Initial intelligence shows local militia forces encountered a small number of enemy combatants while trying to enter the centre of the town."

"Any idea how many?" asked Taylor.

"Reports are sketchy, but several creatures have been spotted near the University of Technology. A number of militia and local soldiers have been wounded, but the enemy appears to make so sign of moving."

She lifted out her Mappad and tapped a button that projected a holographic map in front of them.

"We'll be putting down in this square just one hundred metres from the university. This is not a covert operation. We have superior numbers and firepower. We hit them hard and fast."

"Seems pretty simple," said Silva.

"I want you and Green's platoons to head for the southern entrance. Yorath and Jones, the east side. Taylor and I will take the north side. The only aim of this mission is to eradicate the enemy presence in the shortest time possible, but don't take any unnecessary risks, and no heroics. Remember, the war is over, and this is just clean up work."

"Excuse me, Ma'am, but if the war's over, why are we still fighting?" asked Yorath.

She sighed in response and knew it wasn't an easy thing to answer.

"These are merely skirmishes. There may come a time when we go to war once again, but not today. We don't know if these enemy forces have been left to hinder our operations and rebuilding, or if it was a result of their rapid withdrawal. Either way, remember, those things are dangerous. Keep your platoons tight, and ensure you have superiority of numbers and firepower in any engagement. Any more questions?"

They each studied the map carefully before Green finally spoke up.

"Is this to be our lives for the foreseeable future? Cleaning up the country we have already fought and bled over since this began?"

"Sure is, but it beats hiding in a trench under day long barrages," she replied.

He could not help but agree.

"Alright, good luck to you all, let's move."

Taylor paced alongside Chandra to Rains' copter.

"You surprised as I am that Schulz would be okay with us doing this?" he asked quietly.

"The General has been trying to mend fences ever since you got out of the brig. I suggest you at least appear to be doing the same. The further we get from war conditions, the less you'll get away with."

"And Dupont?"

She sighed at the mere mention of his name.

"He'll always be the same arsehole he always has been. Fortunately, he isn't in command."

"Not of the joint armies no, but let's not forget that we aren't in Germany anymore."

She nodded in agreement and made a mental note to watch out for the French General. He'd been dying to get some payback for some time, and she'd be damned if she would let him.

"This mission, is that all the information we have?" asked Taylor.

"Afraid so. Communication links are still poor, and there isn't the time to investigate further. The civilian population is flooding back into France while it is still littered with dangers. We were not picked because of our investigative abilities. We're a rapid strike force who does not hesitate to jump into combat."

"Well, hell, now you put it like that, I feel all warm and fuzzy inside," he laughed.

She smiled as she could see the genuine relief on the Major's face, now they'd returned to the soldiering they had become so accustomed to.

"How long do you think this will go on?" he asked.

"Oh, I figure we'll have the area cleared within an hour."

"No, I meant this. This taskforce, clearing France of any present dangers."

"With us on the job, not long at all. Why? I thought you wanted to get back in action?"

"Only in place of the shit work we have been doing."

"Lost your stomach for war?" she asked.

"Haven't we all? I didn't think any of us were still here because we enjoyed it."

They went silent as they watched the ground zoom past through the glass of the fuselage. Chandra studied his face, trying to understand where his head was at.

"And if you could be anywhere doing anything, right now, what would it be?" she asked.

"Ah, hell I don't know. I don't know what I want anymore."

She could see he genuinely meant it. They all lived in a world of uncertainty, where the possibility of death was a fear each day.

"Do you really want to keep serving?" she asked.

"What do you mean?"

"You must have served far more years than you ever signed up to. The current war has come to an end, and no one would think lesser of you for wanting to give it all up and go on home."

"And the next war?"

She sighed. "The world fooled itself this last century. Thinking there could ever be an end to war when it is in our nature. There will always be another battle to fight, but there'll be new soldiers to do it."

He sat back and thought about it for a moment. It was the first time he had given some genuine thought to handing in his papers since joining the Corps.

Has it really gotten that bad? He asked himself. He nodded to himself as he answered his own question and continued on.

"Na, I couldn't leave you all now. How could I go home without my friends? This is my family."

"Alright, then, you're stuck with us."

Chandra was contented that Taylor's heart was still in it. She sighed in relief at the thought. She couldn't bear to lose another close friend and ally. The rest of the short journey went by in almost silence as they soared south in the lightning fast copters. Before they had even had time to settle down and rest, Eddie was calling out over the intercom.

"Troyes is up ahead. We'll be landing in two."

Chandra leapt to her feet and took hold of the grab handle above.

"Remember, this is no stand up fight. We're on the hunt. Stay alert, and watch out for traps, bombs and potential ambush zones!" she shouted.

The front thrusters kicked in hard as Eddie brought them in for an abrupt and death defying landing. Taylor could just see out through the cockpit as they narrowly brushed the edge of a tree line and suddenly felt as if the whole craft was cushioned. Chandra rocked to one side but held on firm to the grab handle as the rapid decrease in speed jolted them all forward.

The undercarriage touched down lightly, and Chandra immediately punched the door release.

"Lets go!" she ordered.

They had seen no sign of the enemy, but they all knew how vulnerable they were in a bird on the ground; especially after the roar of their engines would have notified all to their presence. Taylor leapt first from the door, so much so that he missed the ramp and hit the ground running.

His eyes took a moment to adjust to the gleaming light bouncing off the thin sheet of snow that covered the park. He reached an old stone wall and knelt down beside it to survey their surroundings. Silence overcame the area as all crouched and awaited their orders.

Chandra half expected to land in a hot LZ and to have to hit the ground shooting. Despite the relief of the silence, it also made her nervous. She got to her feet and rushed to the wall where Taylor was waiting.

"I don't like this."

"Why? Feels like we're right back to our training scenarios. These are the kind of actions are we trained for. We never expected to be slogging it out in trenches."

"Maybe that's it, what we have become accustomed to. Either way, Mechs fight in open combat, this feels off."

"Aliens invaded our fucking planet. It all feels off."

She smiled in response and was glad of his cool headedness.

"Back when this was a total war, we accepted casualties as a daily part of life. Those days are over, you hear me?" she whispered.

"I hear ya," he replied.

She looked around to the other platoon commanders and nodded for them to continue as planned. The Company arose after just a few hand signals and hushed orders.

Taylor and Chandra advanced just a few metres apart with their platoons surrounding them. They quickly exited the park and were within sight of the university building. The vast complex was in stark contrast to the historical beauty of the stone churches and shopping quarter around it. The walls were of reinforced and mirrored Perspex.

"No visibility in and a hard outer shell, not a bad defensive position," said Taylor.

Chandra drew them to a quick halt as she tried to identify what was on the ground near the entrance. She lifted her rifle and peered down the scope. The body of a dead civilian lay in a pool of blood. It didn't shock her after the bloodshed they had witnessed, but she did sigh at the thought of civilians being killed while trying to rebuild their lives.

"This certainly looks like the place."

She scanned the area and quickly found two trails of blood where human casualties had been dragged away. The ground and building beside the scene had familiar scorch marks where energy pulses had smashed into the stonework.

"Doesn't make any sense," said Taylor.

"I don't think they meant to leave these soldiers behind. They're just trying to survive," replied Chandra.

"You make them sound almost human."

"How would you feel if your armies had left you to die like this?"

She stopped herself as she remembered Taylor's experience of just that. As the shock left his face, he finally nodded in agreement.

"How do you want to play this?" he asked.

"They must surely know we're here, so we have no choice but to hit them hard and quickly."

She tapped her radio mic and was surprised to see it was working.

"No jamming equipment?" she asked in surprise.

"All units breach, go, go, go!"

She leapt to her feet and rushed for the main entrance of the building with the others following closely. Experience of the enemy had taught them to stick close to concentrate their fire. Just as they got within a few metres of the entrance, the Perspex shattered as a pulse ripped through the doors. Chandra rolled and tumbled against a brick wall that surrounded the complex. Taylor smashed into the wall beside him as other pulses rushed overhead.

"Not the best welcome we've ever had!" yelled Taylor.

Gunfire rang out as the Company poured fire into the entrance of the building, bringing down much of the frontage. Taylor peered out from cover and quickly identified the Mechs inside.

"I see three targets. Eleven and one o'clock."

"Looks like they're dug in there pretty good," replied Chandra.

"We could call in a strike, flatten the complex? Not like

there is any risk civilians."

"No, this country has been demolished enough already. The people need some hope that they can return to their old lives."

"Alright, no air support, at least we're used to it now," he replied.

The two of them rose up and fired several controlled bursts into the atrium that was now fully visible from the street. They could make out movement as the Mechs disappeared from sight.

"They're falling back!" Monty called out.

"Forward!" Chandra ordered.

They leapt forward and were quick to utilise the opportunity to get inside. Their boots trampled over the mound of shattered Perspex as it crunched under foot. They reached the long welcome desk from where the Mechs had defended and hunkered down for cover. They expected a continuation of the fight, but the spacious atrium was almost silent as the troops settled down into position.

"Not much of a defence. What the fuck is going on?" whispered Chandra.

"Would you have stood against these odds?"

"Green, report," she asked.

"We've entered the complex, no contact, over."

"Jones, report."

"Light resistance, one enemy down, and we're pursuing

another, over."

She shook her head. "This all just seems too easy."

Taylor nodded in agreement.

"All units proceed with caution."

Taylor stepped up and led his platoon forward with Chandra just a few metres away. He quickly caught sight of a fine trail of blue blood running down a broad corridor further into the huge complex. The two platoons continued after the blood in two columns. The blood trail grew as they reached the entrance to a conference hall. Taylor turned and signalled for them to form up by the entrance. He peered around the doorway and could see the wounded creature laid out on a broad table with the other two trying to stop the bleeding.

The injured creature writhed in pain but made no sound as the other two used what looked like heat torches to seal a wound. The scene made him freeze for a moment. It was eerily reminiscent of scenes that had become familiar to him during the war, but never of the enemy casualties.

He looked away for a moment. He couldn't help but feel it was wrong to try and harm them when they were helping a fallen comrade. For the first time ever, he was beginning to see them as soldiers, rather than faceless aliens. As he sighed at the idea of the death and loss on both sides, his helmet tapped the doorframe. He quickly looked up to see the Mechs inside the room were reaching for their weapons.

Taylor snapped out of his hazy state and jumped through the open doorway. His rifle was firing before his second foot was through the doorway. The first Mech was hit by half a dozen rounds to the chest, and it smashed down onto the hard floor. Just as the other was lifting its weapon to fire, it too was riddled with gunfire from the Major's platoon as one by one they rushed into the hall.

Gunfire ripped through the previously tranquil room as sparks flew, and the last creature finally slumped heavily to the ground. Taylor lowered his rifle and stepped closely towards the wounded Mech on the table. He could see it posed no threat to him and made no attempt to fight.

Chandra stepped through into the room to witness herself what had unfolded. She stopped and gasped at the sight of the creature taking its last few breaths. Its helmet visor was off, and they could see the struggle to breathe until it finally gave up and laid to rest.

"It seems..."

"What?" Taylor asked.

"So human."

Taylor could do nothing but stare at the corpse. The room was silent as the dozen other soldiers who had entered stood solemnly at the bloody sight before them.

"We've got contact, Dining Hall B, floor two!" yelled Jones down the mic.

They could hear gunfire over the transmission and the faint echoes through the building.

"Enough, let's get on mission," whispered Chandra.

They turned and rushed out the door together. Boots echoed down the long corridor as they jogged at the fastest pace they could risk in an urban combat zone. Taylor stopped as he noticed a map of the facilities on a wall beside them.

"Two entrances to that hall, Jones probably went in through the eastern entrance."

"Good, head to the other door. Lead the way!"

He leapt forward and picked up the pace. They were all well aware that it wasn't sensible to rush into danger, but neither could they leave their comrades alone. Taylor reached the stairwell and launched up it three steps at a time. The gunfire was close now. Light seeped out from under a doorway up ahead as the guns roared. The walls were solid; they couldn't see into the room.

Taylor leapt to the other side of the doorway and beckoned for the others to form up either side, ready to breach. Within a second, they were in position.

"Three, two, one! Taylor shouted.

His voice could barely be heard over the battle that was being fought within. He fired two shots into the locking mechanism, as did Lam on the opposite side. The large bore armour-piercing rounds tore through the centre of the double doors, leaving a hole the size of a football.

"Go!" he ordered.

The two of them barged through the door like raging

bulls, forcing the doors to launch from their hinges. Taylor spotted the dug in Mechs immediately and could see they had a good view of the creatures. Despite this, he continued to spread out into the room to allow further troops to join the fight. He rushed up and crouched behind a broad counter, lifting his rifle to fire.

Gunfire cracked behind him, and the advancing troops fired as they passed through the blown entrance. Taylor could see Jones' platoon was dug in the other end of the room and unable to advance. He took aim at the nearest creature. He had a clear view of its flank, fired three rounds into its chest, and a last one through its faceplate as it twitched from the first three. Out of the corner of his eye Mitch could see the other Mechs taking cover.

"Grenades!" he shouted.

He pulled a frag grenade from his webbing and twisted the cap. He looked around to see that three others were waiting for his command.

"Now!"

The four grenades were launched into the air in almost perfect synchronisation and tumbled over into the Mech positions. They hunkered down for cover as the explosions shook the room, and part of the ceiling near them caved in. Taylor jumped up and leapt over the counter top, advancing on the enemy positions with his rifle at the ready.

Chandra looked over the defences to see Mitch had

jumped ahead quicker than any of them were able to follow. She saw him fire two shots into the ground, and as she drew nearer, she could see the body of one of the creatures lying lifeless at his feet. Another lay dead close by. She caught a glimpse of movement, turned quickly, and fired at another creature that was trying to get up from the ground.

She nodded at Mitch, and they both knew each other's thoughts. The grenades were not powerful enough for the enemy they were fighting, and they were not going to take the chance that any had survived. The two officers moved up to the bodies of the other two creatures and fired several rounds through each of their faceplates until they were satisfied it was over.

They stood for a moment, marvelling at their work as Captain Jones approached their positions. Before he could open his mouth, a signal came over their intercom from Lieutenant Green.

"Tracking three hostiles into the basement in the north west of the building, over."

"Hold tight, we're coming," replied Chandra.

She turned and led the way without as much as a word to the troops. As they jogged down the corridors to meet with the others, she noticed specs of blue blood on her arm. Taylor also saw where the spray had coated both of them. He looked at it at first with disgust and then sadness. He was reminded of the scene in the conference hall just minutes before.

Up ahead, they could see Green and Silva, and they had a wounded soldier being attended to.

"Any other casualties?" she asked.

"No, just one wounded. He'll be fine," replied Green.

"Good."

She looked down at the stairwell close by. It appeared to disappear into darkness.

"This where you last saw them?"

"Yes, Ma'am."

"Any other sightings of the enemy?"

He shook his head.

"Jones, you and Yorath are to continue to sweep the rest of this building. Get on it."

The Captain nodded and liaised quickly with Yorath before rushing off to continue his search.

"Any other ways down there?" asked Chandra.

"One fire escape from what I can see."

Taylor looked over at the doorway to a nearby elevator.

"What about that? It goes down below?"

Chandra lifted up her Mappad and carefully studied the limited diagrams they had been given of the layout.

"Not that one, but it looks like there is a freight elevator not far from here."

"I'll take it," replied Taylor.

"Alright, Green you'll take the stairs, but wait for our breach. Silva, you're with me."

Parker had been listening and butted in.

"We can't use that elevator. It will give us away in seconds."

"I don't intend to ride it down," replied Taylor with a smile. "Come on, let's move."

He turned to move out, but Chandra stopped him.

"Confirm when you're in position and ready to go. Green, you wait ten seconds after our breach. That stairwell could be hell."

Taylor nodded in agreement and quickly made his way for the elevator. After passing through a storage area, they found what they were looking for. He drew out his Assegai and thrust it into the join between the doors. The torch style blade cut a hole and broke the seal quickly. He levered open the door and took a look inside.

"Good, it's up on one of the upper floors."

He reached for the emergency stop lever to ensure it stayed put before looking into the most unwelcoming abyss.

"We go down in twos the second we hear that breach, got it?"

They nodded as Parker forced her way to the front. He already knew he could not dissuade her from being the first in.

"We're in position and ready on your signal," he called down the radio.

"All sections ready, we breach in five, four, three…"

replied Chandra.

A small explosion erupted outside the building, and Taylor took it as his cue to jump with Parker at his side. They immediately activated their boosters that lit up the pitch-black shaft as they quickly descended. Taylor ripped open the door, and they could see flashes of light all around; the fight had already begun.

He lifted his rifle and identified one creature as the light reflected from its metallic armour, but Eli had already opened fire. He joined in as the creature was hit with a dozen rounds and killed before it had time to hit the ground. A few more shots rang out until finally all went silent.

"All clear!" yelled Chandra.

Flashlights from friendlies flashed around the room as they all checked for survivors.

Chandra paced up to the fallen creature where Taylor stood.

"What are we doing with the bodies?" he asked.

"Not our problem. We were selected to do the fighting. Clean up work is someone else's job now."

"This was too easy. They can't have been planted here for any resistance, so they must have been left behind."

"Unless by planting them, they intended to continue to cause us the kind of trouble which it is doing. Civilians are scared to go home, soldiers are still busy fighting a war which should be over, and clean up crews are hindered by safety concerns."

"Can't the bastards accept defeat?"

"Would you?"

"Hard to say, but I've never wanted to invade someone else's land and execute them."

A signal came over the radio from Jones.

"Major, the building is secure. All enemy threats have been dealt with."

"Good work, Jones, rendezvous at the boats. Our job here is done."

CHAPTER FIVE

"Damn fine work out there!" shouted Phillips as they lumbered out of the aircraft.

The crowd of nearby troops clapped as they disembarked, but they wondered why. They had done nothing more than their jobs, same as everyone else. General Schulz was also awaiting them, but Dupont was nowhere to be seen. The General strode forward with a broad smile across his face and reached out to shake hands with Chandra and Taylor soon after.

"Glad to see I chose the right soldiers for the job," he exclaimed.

Taylor smirked at the General trying to claim credit for the mission, but he let it slide. One thing he had learnt during the war was that it didn't pay to piss off those in charge. Then he turned to see Parker and Jones and was reminded of why his disobedience to Command had all been worth it.

"Please form up your Company, Major," ordered Schulz.

Chandra looked confused for a moment but turned and bellowed the command. They were all fatigued and wanted nothing more than to sit down in the warm with some hot drinks. She could see the crowd was freezing from awaiting their arrival.

Silly bastard, she thought of Schulz. *Making us all suffer, just for his gratification.*

She took up her position at the forefront of the Company, alongside Taylor and Jones. They were all that remained of the command staff. They watched in amazement as the General stepped up onto a small podium, and a smile stretched across his face at the attention he was garnering. The crowd had already been silenced by the loud shouts of the officers as they formed up. Silva's booming voice had carried across the whole landing zone and drowned out all others. Schulz placed his hands behind his back and stood tall as he finally unleashed his carefully selected speech.

"I want to thank Major Chandra and the 2nd Inter-Allied Company for their continuing efforts in this struggle. Not one among them owes anything to this land, or to my own homelands. And yet, they have given everything to keep them safe. Now they continue to help in every way they can to allow this continent to recover!"

He took a deep breath and an extended pause to allow his words to filter through before continuing. Taylor could see him wallowing in his own self-importance, but it was nothing new.

At least he doesn't want my ass behind bars anymore, thought Taylor.

"No one can doubt the commitment and sacrifices that these fine soldiers have given in duty to the people of this planet. In recognition of their services, President Moreau will be unveiling a monument in their honour. Major Chandra, it is my pleasure to request the presence of your company for this ceremony at 1000 hours tomorrow."

Chandra stared at the General in shock. It appeared as if Schulz was expecting to see some gratitude from her, but she couldn't help but feel that it was a pointless publicity stunt they were being drawn into when there was real work to be done. She strained to smile in response.

"Thank you, Sir," she replied.

Schulz looked put out by her short and passive response, but he would not let it ruin his moment of glory.

"I am sure you are all eager to get some rest. Well done to all of you. Thank you all for your continued service!"

He began to clap and was soon joined by all who were present. Taylor could not help but feel sorry for all the personnel around them who had been drawn into Schulz's plan. They deserved credit as much as the Inter-Allied did. Chandra saluted before turning and dismissing the troops.

Schulz saluted them as they left, in a gesture that was so blatantly staged. Taylor stepped up to Chandra's side as they finally plodded on.

"Will we never be rid of him?" he asked.

"Not likely. He's always miles from the action."

Taylor nodded in agreement.

"Schulz aside, that was good work today, to complete a mission without losing a single soldier. I was wondering if we'd ever see the day."

* * *

The Company stood formed up beside a podium and what was some kind of monument still under wraps. Chandra paced up and down the line as they awaited the arrival of the French President and the other officials who were to honour them that day.

Opposite them stood a hundred strong youth marching band in gleaming dress uniforms. She looked back at her own troops and could see they had done their very best to look presentable, but there was no hiding their well worn and fatigued combat uniforms. She could see rips in fabric; cuts and scrapes on faces where shrapnel had left many scarred.

She smiled at the stark contrast of her battle-hardened unit to the gleaming presentation that had been set up for then. She preferred them that way. They presented themselves as they were; the few who were tough enough and lucky enough to have survived the war.

The Drum Major lifted his baton, and the band's silence was broken as the brass and drums rang out around them. Chandra turned to see a motorcade approaching with French armoured vehicles at the forefront. Every vehicle proudly flew the French tricolor in a colourful entrance. She turned and looked in astonishment at the absurdity of the event.

Within a fifty metre radius was nothing but an impeccable parade display, but it was just one pocket of perfection amongst the ruins of the city that lay all around them. Beyond that lay massive cranes stretching up into the skyline. Only two buildings over five storeys high had survived the brutal struggle for the city, and they could see for kilometres.

Taylor caught sight of Chandra turning as she marvelled at the sights around them. They both knew they had been there before, but it was hard to recognise much of the city any longer. Chandra drew the Company to attention as the vehicles drew near, and they watched as the cheery President waved from his car.

On one hand, Taylor felt sorry for the French leader for having lost so much of his country, but on the other hand, he looked at the man's impeccable clothing and well fed stomach and scowled at how little he had put into the war. Chandra could see the look of disgust on his face and strolled over to whisper beside him.

"Major, I know you're not one for authority, but let's not fuck this up, you hear?"

"He's gonna stand there and talk about our shared struggle to free these lands. What did he ever do?" snapped Taylor.

"We all have our part in this, not all of it is holding a rifle and fighting on the frontline," she replied.

He nodded in agreement and could feel some of the anger seep away.

"I'm just sick of it all, those bastards, Schulz and Dupont. They toss us about as assets, and then want to take all the glory."

"Hey, this here is for us, don't you forget that. The President has a responsibility to the people of this country, and he is clearly fulfilling that. Cut the man some slack, you have no idea what his part was in this war."

Chandra saluted as the car drew to a halt and watched as President Moreau leapt out and up towards the podium. The two Majors stared in astonishment for a moment. They had never met the French President, but they knew from news feeds that he was a much older man than the one who was about to address them. Commander Phillips approached them in full number one dress.

"Sir, that, that isn't the President," stated Chandra.

"It is now, Major. President Moreau passed away a week ago from a heart attack. The government decided in the interest of the people that his son should take over to allow the population to have someone they can relate to."

"That ain't very democratic," replied Taylor from the sideline.

Chandra turned and smiled to see that Mitch had crept closer to listen in.

"No, but what else were they to do? Not like they could start an e-vote and have it done by the weekend. Communications in this country are still an utter shambles."

"What's he like, this new President?"

"Driven. He's a high roller and vicious to boot. He's got balls and has no problem walking over people to get ahead."

"Sounds about right," replied Taylor.

"But maybe not the right man for the job. These people need somebody with empathy. Somebody who can hold them together, not drive them apart," whispered Chandra.

"I'd hold your tongue, Major," replied Phillips. "We're soldiers, not politicians. The two don't mix well."

They fell silent as Moreau stepped up to the podium, without introduction from the speaker who stepped aside speechless. The President lifted his hand, and the band quickly faded off into silence. He looked out across the lines of British and American soldiers and to the civilians who had gathered for the ceremony. Only a hundred Parisians had turned out for the event, but many soldiers from European armies were scattered amongst them.

"Men and Women of France, and of the world, we gather here among the ruins of our fine capital city not to mourn our losses, but to celebrate our victories! The soldiers of the Second Inter-Allied Company have served the world and given everything they had to make this land free!"

Whistles and clapping burst out from the audience, but Taylor felt nothing. He didn't ask for any praise for what they had done. He didn't want any medals or awards. He turned back to look at Eli's face. As he glanced at her with wide eyes, she noticed and turned to meet his. She smiled before turning as she blushed. The President lifted up his hand again and nodded in acknowledgement, as if he himself were being applauded for the victory.

"It is my pleasure and honour to reveal this monument to the world. It stands as an eternal reminder of the sacrifices made by these fine men and women."

He pointed for the men waiting on the ropes next to the covered monument that stood ten metres high. The soft cloth rolled off the hard stone, and they looked in awe at what lay beneath. The base was of a thick stone column and atop it was a character stood with one foot on the body of a fallen alien. Taylor instantly recognised that it was a homage to his defeat over Karadag. The statue of him was thrusting an Assegai into the air triumphantly.

"St George slaying the Dragon," whispered Chandra.

"What?" asked Taylor who was still in a daze.

"That's what you have become, the people's hero. That's you."

Taylor went silent. He was humbled by the towering figure of himself. Clapping rang out from the Company behind them and was soon joined by everyone in attendance. He turned to see the troops were alive with excitement, but he could not help feel that it did them an injustice.

"Why've they got to choose me? Any soldier who fought in this war has reason to be up there."

Chandra laughed. "People need something positive to hang on to. It's a David and Goliath story which is symbolic of our entire struggle."

"I never wanted to be on no statue," he snapped.

"It's not about you, Mitch. People need hope, and you just happened to have become the poster boy. Let them have this, they need it."

He turned and looked back at the imposing figure of himself towering over them all.

Is this what I am destined to be? A celebrity? He asked himself.

The day continued with the same surreal display of celebrations. Lights and music blared out, but Taylor could not help but look away into the desolate wasteland of the city. He felt overwhelmed by it all. It was too soon to be celebrating among the ruins that were the final resting place of so many fellow soldiers. Taylor's ears suddenly twitched as he heard the ring of a communicator nearby.

He turned to see Phillips pull out the device from his pocket.

"Excuse me, Gentlemen," he said as he turned away and took a few paces to answer the call. Taylor watched intently as he could see the Commander's face turn from the pleasant festivities to the calculating officer he had been throughout the conflict. He spoke for little over a minute before quickly pushing his way to the podium. Taylor tapped Chandra's shoulders and pointed to the commotion.

"Guess that'll be for us then," she mused.

The Commander reached the centre podium and leaned in to mutter a few words to the President before stepping forward with a megaphone in one hand.

"Can I have your attention, please!" called Phillips.

The loudhailer spread for miles out across the open desolate ground.

"The Second Inter-Allied command staff are to report immediately to me at HQ. The rest of the Company is to gear up and assemble at landing zone alpha in thirty minutes. Transport is en route. Get moving!"

Sighs rang out among the ranks as they quickly broke formation and headed for the convoy of trucks trundling towards them.

"My sincerest apologies to President Moreau and everyone else who has made it here today. On behalf of the Company, I'd like to thank you all for your tremendous support, and the manner in which you have honoured the fine men and women of the Inter-Allied today. Thank you and good luck with your continuing efforts."

The Commander turned and whispered a few words to the President, shook his hand, and leapt from the podium. Taylor and Chandra were awaiting him with Jones rapidly approaching. The Commander pointed for them to follow as he rushed past them.

"What's going on, Sir?" insisted Chandra.

"I don't have much yet. All I know is there is a situation which your team is being requested for."

"Sounds ominous," she replied.

"If it wasn't, they'd not be calling for you."

"Always we land in the shit," muttered Taylor.

"You said it, Major. In the shit situations is where you have proven to excel, so get used to them."

Taylor laughed at the notion.

* * *

Phillips quickly scanned the information as Taylor and Chandra stood calmly before him. He shook his head as he read further and finally looked up with a sigh.

"Time is not on our side here, so I'm going to be brief. Not like I have a wealth of information to pass on anyway. There is an ongoing incident here, in Dijon."

He pointed to the city that they could see was around

three hundred kilometres southeast of Paris. Yet more ground they were utterly unfamiliar with.

"Police who were returning to the area found one of their precincts occupied by remaining enemy forces. Along with members of the Gendarmerie, they have surrounded the complex and initiated a siege."

"Then why do they need us?" asked Chandra.

"This is more than they can handle, Major. After the terror attacks fifty years ago, many such buildings were reinforced as protection from bombs and high explosive projectile launchers."

"And I'm guessing they didn't stay to defend these fortresses during the war?" snapped Taylor.

"That's just the thing."

"Ah, great," whispered Chandra.

"When the mass hysteria set in, and the roads turned to shit, many key members of the local authorities took shelter in a bunker built beneath the city, along with anyone too frail to make it the distance. As far as we know, they're still down there. We can't bomb this building, as we simply have no idea what it'd be willing to withstand."

The door to the HQ room burst open. They quickly turned to see Captain Jones in full combat attire with the two Majors' equipment hanging from each arm.

"We're ready to move," he stated.

Chandra grasped her gear from Jones. The immense weight that included the exo suit hulked to the ground with a resounded crash. She turned back to Phillips as she began to gear up.

"Anything else? Enemy strength? Casualties?"

"Sorry. The emergency distress call was cut off in what is reminiscent of the jamming we saw during the war. Local forces say they have surrounded the facility but had sustained casualties and were unable to make progress."

"Great, we're going in almost blind," she replied.

"You should be used to it by now," said Taylor.

Chandra nodded as she gritted her teeth. It wasn't a helpful comment, but it didn't make it any less true. She turned to Jones and quickly snapped out her orders.

"Be ready for lift off the second we reach you."

Charlie nodded and quickly rushed out of the room to make final preparations. She looked back to Taylor and could see that he was equally as unimpressed with their intelligence and going into yet another blind operation.

"Commander, we may punch above our weight, but what happens if we come across enemy resistance beyond the stragglers we have seen so far? With no intelligence and restrictions in our air support, we could be left to die."

"I won't let that happen, Major." He paced a few steps but turned back.

"The truth is this country is a God damn mess. They're too few troops and workers to get everything done. Now that the war's over, few are interested, and many are stuck trying to rebuild their own countries. The only reason you and me are here is because the UK remained relatively untouched by the whole affair."

"We're not the only team like this, are we?" asked Taylor.

Chandra watched in astonishment as the Commander shook his head in response.

"No, but you are the most successful. Enemy resistance is being found all over in the lands which were the fighting grounds of this war."

"That's half the bloody world," she said.

Phillips nodded.

"Taskforces have been set up all over to try and deal with them. There are two other units like you in France alone. Some have had it a lot worse."

"How much worse?" Taylor asked.

"Enough to cause some of those units to be withdrawn from service and have to be replaced. The war may be over, but we are still burning through troops."

Taylor moaned. "You'd think it was time the French Army took over the job in its own country," he spat.

"That may well be so, but there are too few of them left as it is. This country needs our help just as much as ever. After all, what was the point in fighting, if we were just going to leave them to the wolves at the very end?"

"I thought we were fighting for our survival, not for France."

"That's enough!" shouted Chandra.

Phillips could not bring himself to discipline Taylor for

his outrageous behaviour. Not only did he support Mitch's opinion, but also fully appreciated the fact that they were the ones having to do the fighting.

"We know everything there is to know. Every second we waste here now puts further lives in danger. With your permission, Sir, we're moving out."

"Good luck, Major, to both of you and all of the Company."

Taylor nodded as a thank you. He had calmed once it became apparent there was nowhere left to vent his anger.

"Let's move," said Chandra.

The two officers pulled on their helmets and rushed out of the room to find the copters loaded and ready to go, just as Chandra had requested. Jones stood on the entry ramp to one, beckoning for her to join him.

"I'll see you on the ground!" shouted Taylor.

He split off and rushed for one of the other copters where he could see Parker waiting for him. Even before his foot was through the door, the engines were roaring to life. He leapt into the craft and slumped in a seat that had been left for him. Parker rested down beside him as the thrusters lifted them off the ground.

"Guess this is the same as last time?" she asked.

"Pretty much."

He looked to the rest of his platoon who barely seemed to care for further information, but he was going to tell them anyway.

"Listen up. We're going in hot, hotter than our previous mission. As to be expected, we've got barely any intelligence for the area and little understanding of what faces us. All we do know is that civilian and local forces are on the ground and having a hard time. Air support is unfeasible due to friendlies held up beneath the enemy positions."

"Beneath them?" asked Clark.

"Some kind of bunker, and that's all we know."

"Great. So we can't flatten it, we have multiple civilians involved, and a dug in enemy?" replied Lam.

"You got it," replied Taylor with a smile.

It was a short journey to Dijon when they were in the air, but it was yet another tedious trip in a post-war environment that seemed more miserable and desperate than the hardships that preceded it.

"Landing in five!" called Rains over the intercom.

Taylor opened his mouth to speak but was instantly silenced as their copter took a heavy impact, jerking them harshly.

"Incoming, incoming!" Rains shouted.

Their copter took quick evasive action and banked heavily as the engines roared to full power. Taylor felt his heart stop at the realisation that this was already not going to be half as simple as he'd hoped.

"We've got pulses incoming. I can't shake 'em!" Eddie called out.

A second later, the ship rocked again even harder, and a hole ripped through the fuselage. They were fortunately at a low enough altitude that they stayed in their seats.

"This is echo five, we are going down. I repeat, going down."

Taylor could feel they were descending quickly, and Eddie was having a hard time getting the nose up as they plummeted towards the ground. He looked around at the other marines and could see there was little fear in their faces. No one cried out in fright or panicked. They knew their fate was out of their hands. They expected to hit the ground at any minute, but then the copter rocked back as thrusters kicked in. It was not enough to slow their descent completely, and just a few seconds later they crashed through the outer wall of a vast industrial complex.

Taylor grasped the grab handles tightly beside him and held Parker with his other hand as their transport smashed down to the ground and slid fifty metres along the ground, smashing everything aside in its wake. Sparks flew several metres high either side of them until they finally rocked to a sudden halt.

They looked around at each other in astonishment, not one of them had been injured. They could do nothing for a moment but remain in their seats in shock and disbelief. Eddie leapt into the cabin with a smile on his face.

"Well, holy shit, that ain't the most graceful manoeuvre of my career."

Taylor and Parker began to laugh reservedly until the rest joined them. The Major got to his feet and reached forward to shake Eddie's hand.

"Damn fine flying, Lieutenant."

"Really? Where'd you learnt to fly?"

"Joking aside, you just saved our asses."

"I'll remind you of that."

"I'm sure."

Taylor strode to the door and hit the release button, but it didn't respond. He lifted his leg and kicked with the force of his exo-suit, and the door burst from its mechanism and slid out across the concrete floor outside. He coughed for a minute as thick dust filled his mouth. As it cleared, he looked out across the plant floor and could see the body shells of hundreds of cars and the wake of many more that they had trashed.

"Eddie, the insurance companies will love you."

The Lieutenant reached the door and jumped out with the Major to walk among the wreckage. He spun around, marvelling at his work until a broad smile appeared on his face once again.

"It's okay. They're French cars, so they were scrap to begin with!"

Taylor chuckled as he leapt from the door and landed with a heavy thud on the hard floor.

"As for my baby, look at her!" shouted Eddie.

"Any chance of salvaging the work you have done?" he

replied.

"Salvaging? Fuck yeah, you think I'm gonna leave this marvel of technology for the locals?"

Taylor tapped his intercom.

"Major Chandra, please come in."

There was no reply for a moment, and he quickly repeated his request as the troops flooded out of the crash site.

"This is Chandra. We thought you were goners, Major."

"Close to it, but we're still standing."

"Any casualties?" she asked.

Taylor shook his head in surprise. "Amazingly, no. We're ready to continue on mission."

"Got it. The other bird went down hard. We're at the crash site now. Two dead, eight wounded."

"Fuck," Taylor whispered to himself.

There was silence for a moment as Chandra stepped out of earshot of the troops, so she could talk more privately.

"Mitch, this mission must go on. With defences like this, there must be something damn important down there. We'll be a little while here attending to the wounded. You'll have to get yourselves to Dijon. We'll be with you ASAP."

"Got it."

"And, Mitch, watch your arse. This is not the Troyes mission. Maybe that drew us into a false sense of security. We've already lost people over this, so let's not loose anymore, hey?"

"I hear you."

"Good luck, Major, we'll see you shortly, over and out."

He turned and looked up to see that Eli had been stood behind him listening.

"In the shit as usual, then?"

He nodded as he lifted his Mappad and identified their location in relation to the city.

"Alright, everyone listen up!"

Taylor looked out to see they were already awaiting his orders as they marvelled at the wreckage of the copter they had crash-landed in. The fuselage had been ripped apart when it crashed through the car production lines and machinery. He looked at the twisted wreckage for a moment and turned back to them.

"Major Chandra is assisting at the other crash site. We've got two dead already, and this fight hasn't even started yet. For now, we're on our own. We're about forty kilometres out from our destination and without transport. This mission does not stop because we hit a complication."

None of them showed any sign of surprise by his orders. He could see in their faces that more than anything they wanted their pound of flesh for the losses they had already suffered.

"Parker, find us suitable transport that'll get us all to Dijon ASAP."

"Not gonna be easy."

"Appreciated, do what you can."

"On it," she replied.

She nodded to her platoon to follow her as they headed for the nearest exit in search of wheels.

"Eddie, you're gonna have to come with us. You got gear with you?"

"Armour and a rifle, but nothing like the shit you use."

"It'll do, gear up and be ready to move."

"Always wanted to join the Marine Corps," he jested.

Taylor nodded in gratitude as the pilot's laid back and lax attitude seeped away and was replaced by a professional soldier.

"Sir?" asked Lam.

"Go."

"Even if Sergeant Parker can find a vehicle, how are we going to make it through on the ground? It's taken us days to clear some roads."

"True, but civilians are clearly getting through to Dijon. We're north east of the city, and the roads we'll be using must have already been made passable."

"And the bird?" asked Williams, pointing to the crashed copter.

"We'll leave it to recovery crews. We can't destroy something so valuable. I doubt anyone will come looking for it yet. Remember, we aren't in hostile territory anymore. These are free lands."

"Could have fooled me," snapped Lam.

Taylor nodded. "I know. But remember, there's a big difference between fighting an insurgency and a war. If anything, this is what we did have experience of before the war started."

Rains leapt from the wreckage with his body armour half on and a rifle in hand. His bandana was still firmly around his head, and Taylor could already tell it would be futile to ask him to remove it.

"Alright, outside now. Let's see what Parker has got us."

They marched out of the complex to find Parker's platoon stood around an articulated car transporter. Thick dust and dirt coated the polymer body of the cab, and they could see rust bubbling down much of the steelwork of the frame of the trailer.

"Jesus, you couldn't find anything smaller?" yelled Rains.

Parker spun around.

"It's the only thing left on site that works, or at least we hope works. Looks like it hasn't been used in a few years."

"Few years? Shit, I haven't seen one of these in a long time," replied Eddie.

She stepped aside to reveal two of her unit working on a side panel of the truck. A few seconds later, the engine fired up. The bodywork shook as the old engine rattled on its mounts.

"Jesus, that thing even going to make it?"

"It's fuel cell driven by the old b-cells, Lieutenant. The

reason we can get the fuel, is it's the only thing nobody else would want around here. The old building heaters run off it, but that's about it."

"I'd call it a stroke of luck, but that would be pushing it," Taylor grinned.

"Improvise and overcome, hey, Major?" she replied with a smile.

He turned to his platoon and gestured forward.

"All aboard!"

122

CHAPTER SIX

A sign on the edge of the road read 'Bienvenue a Dijon'. Cheers rang out along the open carriage of the vehicle as they roared past. It was some of the only French they recognised. In the war torn country, it was rare to see signs still standing. As they breezed past, they could see it had been smashed down and was now propped up by several pieces of rough timber and lashed together.

"At least they got it back up," said Taylor.

"Doesn't that just say everything about this situation? Civilians rushing back into a warzone before it's been made safe. Causing more trouble than they're solving?" Hall asked.

"Can you blame them? All they want is their lives back."

They could barely hear each other over the wind noise. They estimated Parker must be running the truck at over a hundred kilometres an hour.

"You know if she crashes this thing, we're all gonna die."

"All the life threatening situations we've been in, and now you decide to consider the risk?" Taylor replied.

They both laughed as they soared towards the city. Their faces turned sour as they spotted two thin wisps of black smoke arising up ahead. Taylor turned back to see the grim but professional faces of all those with them. Eddie was the only one among them who smiled. Taylor wondered if he'd just not experienced the horrors they had yet, but he suspected it was more a brave face put on for the others' benefit.

Up ahead, they caught a glimpse of a police cruiser at the side of the road with two officers stood in the road. Parker brought the vehicle to a halt. The brakes squealed and hissed and made them wonder if she'd even tried them out during the entire trip. The two cops looked in surprise as the vehicle drew up in front of them, and they could make out the soldiers on top of the trailer. They walked around to talk to the driver, but Taylor shouted down from above.

"Major Taylor, 2nd Inter-Allied. We're here to help."

The two cops were stunned for a moment as they tried to comprehend what they could see.

"This all? You all that's coming?"

"For now. We were shot down en route to you."

"That was you? So much for reinforcements."

Taylor groaned at the lack of appreciation. "If you don't mind, we've got a job to do."

"By all means, but you're going to need more than your bunch to fight this battle, Monsieur."

Taylor nodded with gritted teeth. He wanted nothing more than to jump down and punch the man's teeth out, but he restrained himself.

"Parker, let's go!" he shouted.

The truck rocked forward with just enough time for the two cops to step aside and marvel at the rusting hulk trundling past. The marines glared at the men who wouldn't show them an ounce of gratitude or respect. Hall wanted to spit on them for their ignorance and rudeness, but he felt Taylor's hand on his shoulder and knew he must remain civil.

"What have those fuckers been doing the whole war? Waiting for us to turn up and do all the bloody work?"

"It sucks, but look at it from their perspective. They expected their country and their government to protect them. They have lost almost everything they have. What is the upside? Would you be all cheery in their shoes?"

"I think I'd show a little fucking gratitude. This isn't even our God damn country!"

"I hear, ya," replied Taylor.

They passed through dozens of quiet streets, seeing only a handful of civilians here and there. Then Parker's voice rang out from the cab.

"Major! Take a look at this!"

He stood up on the top of the trailer that stretched up over the roof of the truck, grasping the rail beside him as the vehicle glided towards the horrific sight ahead. They could see a dozen filled body bags at the side of the road and medics working a way beyond with several dozen more casualties. A number of other wounded and bloodied soldiers and policemen lay about on benches and walls all around. Parker drew the vehicle to a halt once again as they reached the bloody scene.

Taylor leapt from the high trailer, descending five metres. He hit the ground hard but balanced, and with the suit taking the impact from his joints. Several troops looked up in curiosity. It was clear they had never seen such advanced equipment before. He looked to the doctor who was busy patching up a wounded woman.

As he panned quickly across the scene, he spotted one soldier with sergeant's stripes whose arm was bound up, but otherwise he looked okay. Mitch quickly strolled up to the man. Few seemed to care to utter a word to them.

"Sergeant, we're here to help, but we need to know the current situation."

The man looked up with staring eyes. Taylor could see straight into the man's troubled mind. He'd given up and lost hope. He didn't even try to utter a word. Mitch had no tolerance for his attitude. He could already tell he wasn't going to get anywhere with words. He took two brisk paces forward and slapped the man hard across the face. The Sergeant's head snapped around from the heavy-handed strike.

The wounded at the scene were frozen in shock for just a few seconds before half a dozen reached for their guns and trained them on the Major. They were targeted by half of Taylor's platoon before their weapons were even raised. Mitch stood calm, tall and still empty handed. The whole street had gone quiet as the newcomers faced off against the locals.

"I am Major Mitch Taylor. I have been sent here, under the command of Major Chandra, in a relief force that targets all remaining pockets of enemy resistance. We are here to help, so I expect at least a little co-operation!"

A few whispers spread across the wounded men and women. Taylor could only make out one word among their French that he recognised, 'immortels'. The Sergeant he had slapped stood up carefully, looking Taylor up and down to see if he truly stood before the soldiers who had risen to such fame. He turned and lifted his hand, gesturing for the others to lower their weapons.

"Major, you will forgive our lack of hospitality. We have suffered greatly trying to take this city back."

"And we have been suffering since the day this war began. We've already had two killed and more wounded just trying to reach you. Give us any info you have, and we'll be on our way to get this mess cleared up."

Mitch could see it pained the Sergeant to be so belittled by them, but he wasn't going to fight it.

"Our Captain is still at the front. We encircled the police station but so far have been unable to gain any ground within. They've got a lot of firepower, and we cannot risk any bombardment because of the civilians in a bunker below."

"I am well aware of the bunker, Sergeant. Any idea on the enemy strength?"

"We've counted a couple of dozen, but there could be more. Just follow this road straight, and you'll find the action."

Taylor nodded in gratitude for the assistance, but he wished he hadn't had to fight to get it out of their allies. He paced back to the truck and stepped up onto the footplate beside the passenger door of the cab.

"Take us forward."

Within a couple of minutes, they had the station in sight and could make out the dug in positions of the French forces.

"Stop here, Sergeant. We'll go it on foot."

The vehicle rocked to a halt. Parker tapped the dash twice with a smile, as a thank you for the old truck having got them there. Taylor stepped off the side of the vehicle and strode casually forward. His weapon was resting low across his body, but his hands grasped it in readiness.

Taylor's platoon quickly formed up behind him and

continued down the street in two columns either side. Mitch himself defiantly strode down the centre as if he had no care for his life. In fact, he only did so to show his confidence and survey the ground ahead. He could already tell they were still a way behind the friendly defences.

No gunfire rang out, nor the screams and shouts of combat. They could see a dozen soldiers dug in behind a barrier of cars ahead. Most of them sat back against the vehicles and watched Taylor approached. There had clearly been a lull in the fighting. Mitch could tell the will to fight amongst the remaining troops had been utterly sapped away. He approached confidently while carefully studying everything in front of him.

There were scorch marks in the surrounding buildings and cars that were being used as cover. One had completely burnt out to a blackened shell. Between their defences and the entrance to the station were the bodies of three French soldiers. It was a grim thing to see, but he'd been conditioned to such a degree that it didn't faze him anymore.

"Who's in charge here?" he shouted.

There was no response by the demoralised troops. Some looked away, and others were still captivated by the equipment they wore. Taylor paced right up to their position and stopped just two metres from the line. Finally, one spoke.

"Captain Fournier, 4th Hussars Squadron, and you

are?"

"Major Taylor, 2nd Inter-Allied Company."

"Of what regiment?"

"To be quite honest, I don't know anymore, Captain. We've been merged with so many allies that there is no other way to identify us any longer. All I can tell you is that we form one of the taskforces established for this kind of work."

The Captain looked down and sighed with a dismissive grin.

"I believe you, Major, I really do. But what can you do here? They're dug in with substantial firepower. We have seen at least two-dozen Mechs, and there are probably a good many more. We'd need another two hundred soldiers to get this done."

Two lights flashed up ahead, and Taylor instantly recognised them as enemy gunfire.

"Cover!" he shouted.

The heat pulses rushed overhead past the blockage just a split second after they had hit the ground. Parker's back smashed against an over turned car, and she looked up just in time to see one of the pulses burst through the windshield of the transporter that had carried them there in safety. The glass shattered and the interior quickly caught fire.

"God damn bastards!"

She watched as flames engulfed the truck and smoke

rose through the street. It only served to make her hungrier for blood.

"Captain! Have they tried to break out at all, or are they staying put?" asked Taylor.

"They aren't moving anywhere. I tried pulling back to encourage them out, but they don't want to leave," he replied.

Mitch peered up over the bonnet of the vehicle they were using for cover to see several Mech gun barrels protruding from windows. He couldn't think of a safe way of attacking with what they had.

"How many men do you have?" he asked the Captain.

"Still left at the defences, about eighty."

Taylor shook his head. "We need more."

The Captain nodded as if to say it was obvious.

Taylor's communicator crackled as a signal came through.

"Major Taylor, come in."

Taylor smiled as he recognised Chandra's voice. "This is Taylor."

"What is your situation?"

"We are in position at the perimeter, heavy resistance inside. We are unable to breach at current strength."

"Good work. We're en route. We breach from the roof in three minutes. Be ready."

"Got it."

He turned back to the combined troops who were

scattered in a ragtag line where they had hurried to cover.

"Help is on the way. Check your weapons. We move in three."

The Captain turned in shock and grabbed the Major's shoulder to pull him around into eye contact.

"Major, what the hell are you doing? We can't assault! It's suicide!"

"We aren't doing this alone. We don't move until the attack is underway. We should be able to advance under the chaos of what's coming."

"And what is coming?"

"The Immortals."

The man's eyes lit up as he instantly recognised the name and remembered hearing of Major Taylor in regard to them. He lifted his rifle and looked up over the barricade as he relayed the information to his men through their radio systems. Two minutes later, they suddenly heard the roar of engines approaching quickly from the north. They could hear whatever was closing was skimming the rooftops, and the engines were booming through the streets.

"This is it, ready!" shouted Taylor.

A copter roared overhead and deafened them as the reverse thrusters kicked in. A dust cloud blinded them for a second, and they wondered if the aircraft even had enough clearance over the station. Through the thick dust they saw the lights of suit thrusters glare as Chandra's troops descended quickly onto the rooftop. Gunfire rang out as they quickly overcame whatever sentries were atop the building. Mitch looked over to see the look of both shock and hope in the Frenchmen.

"Let's go!" he ordered.

Taylor's coarse voice roared out and was heard by most, even over the boomed engines of the hovering copter. He leapt over the car and hit the ground running. As soon as he saw the first pulses of energy rushing towards them, he wished they'd had the shields with them. Intelligence had made it clear that their missions were low risk, rapid raids and not the vicious gun battles they had become so accustomed to.

"Fuck me!" he screamed as he felt the burn of a pulse rush past his head.

He opened fire as he ran, puncturing holes in the reinforced glass of the doors to the station. The soldiers all around him joined in the action, and the ground floor of the building was devastated by a volley of fire. He leapt over the body of one of the fallen soldiers from the previous fight and ducked down at the base of the wide flight of steps leading to the entrance.

"Grenades!"

He doubted anyone would have heard him, but they'd understand. He twisted the firing cap of a high explosive charge and launched it through the entrance. He ducked down as five more were thrown through the breach.

Seconds later, an explosion rang out which was echoed by several more. Smoke and dust burst out from the doorways and left the entrance in a haze.

"Advance!"

They leapt to their feet and rushed through the building entrance. Parker and several others had managed to get ahead and were already blazing away before he'd gotten through what remained of the doors. Gunfire rang out, but had already silenced by the time he got through the dust cloud. Three Mechs lay dead on the ground. He turned to see three of the Frenchmen had been killed on the assault, and two of his wounded; their lives saved by Reiter's armour. They could hear gunfire still raging on the floors above.

"Alright, let's get this building cleared. Parker, you are to sweep and clear the ground floor. Fournier, your task is to go to the aid of the bunker and get those civilians out to safety. We're heading up to assist Major Chandra. Let's go!"

The three groups quickly split apart. Only seconds after Parker's platoon had left his sight, and Taylor could hear pulses and gunfire where they had met opposition. For just a second, he stopped and hesitated about leaving her to assist the others. He knew he had a responsibility to remain professional, no matter their relationship, but he could not help but feel cold for leaving her in combat.

"What is it?" asked Lam.

Taylor shook his head as he snapped out of it.

"Nothing, let's keep moving."

They rushed up the stairs at a rapid pace, covering three steps in every leap. Taylor ripped open the door to the first floor to be met by a line of a half dozen Mechs waiting for them.

"Down!" he screamed.

He leapt from the doors, just in time to miss a pulse heading for his face. Another clipped the edge of his waistline armour and burning a few millimetres from it. Williams was unconscious on the ground where a pulse had hit him full force in the chest. Mitch prayed he was still alive, but there was nothing he could do for him in that moment.

"What the fuck are we gonna do now, Sir?" shouted Lam.

He peered around to see that there was only one entrance on that floor, and they couldn't reach the other side of the stairway without crossing the path of fire. The Mechs continued to fire odd shots through the entrance, but they didn't appear to be advancing.

Taylor got to his feet and leapt over to the sidewall they had passed getting to the door, where several from his platoon were huddled. He tapped the wall with his knuckles, trying to estimate its strength.

"We need a new entrance."

Lam smiled, understanding the Major's idea.

"Clear the way," ordered Taylor.

He and Lam trained their weapons on the centre of the wall and fired a dozen shots between them. They lowered their weapons to see they had blasted a half metre hole into the room the other side, and several cracks had spread around the breach. Without any further thought, Taylor charged like a raging bull and launched himself at the breach. To their amazement the wall caved in with his weight, and he tumbled through into the room.

"Fuck, that's awesome," stated Lam.

Taylor rolled onto one knee and beckoned them to follow him through.

"Clark, stay here with four others. Lay down some covering fire while we flank 'em," whispered Taylor.

Contented that his plan was underway, Taylor turned his attention to the room and making sure they were safe. He stood up and slowly crept up to the entrance door. A small glass window at eye level afforded him a good view beyond. The room led to a typical two metre wide corridor that ran throughout the floor. He turned back to see the last of his marines were climbing through. He signalled for them to join him.

"I reckon this corridor will lead straight to the stair and elevator hall where those bastards are dug in."

"Think we can work our way around the floor and hit 'em from behind?" asked Lam.

Taylor took a deep breath, breathing out through his

nose with a sigh as he gave it some thought.

"Maybe. But I don't want to risk getting hit by our covering fire, and I want this done quickly. We get out into that corridor, and we don't stop moving until we hit them hard."

The marines nodded in agreement. Taylor lifted his weapon, pulled out the magazine, and slammed in a fresh one. Lam quickly followed suit. Neither of them wanted to go in without the maximum firepower they could bring to bear. Mitch opened the door and stepped cautiously out into the corridor. He quickly looked both ways and could see no sign of movement. He stepped over to the opposite wall and a few metres in the enemy direction, stopping to wait for the others.

As soon as they were clear of the room, Taylor signalled for them to move forward. They clung to the sidewalls of the corridor in two columns. Taylor led the right side. He could feel his heart pounding once again. The danger was always most apparent in the calm before the storm.

Taylor reached the bend at the end of the corridor and lifted his fist to stop them briefly. They could clearly hear the pulses firing now. He edged around the corner just enough to get a clear view. The creatures were waiting in the open atrium with no cover to use at all. He smiled as he realised his plan had come together, and they had caught them utterly by surprise.

Mitch turned to his marines and nodded to give the go

ahead. He lifted three fingers as a countdown. As soon as the third finger was dropped, their weapons were lifted to the shoulder, and they were ready to rush. The second finger went down and Taylor took a deep breath to calm him. Finally, it was time. The last finger went down, and he leapt from the corner into the open atrium.

There was no hesitation from the marines as they opened fire the second they had a target. Ten shots smashed into the Mechs before they had time to turn to face the new threat, and their bodies spasmed with multiple shots piercing their armour. From the stairway door, Taylor could see muzzle flashes rage, and the other marines rush in to join in the slaughter. The Mechs only managed two shots between them as they were riddled with armour piercing rounds. The pulses smashed into the walls with no effect as the creatures were killed where they stood.

Taylor's marines didn't stop closing the distance but rushed all the way up to the enemy position, so they could stand over their vanquished enemy and fire a few more shots into the creatures while they were down. The room went quiet for just a moment as they marvelled at their work. The silence was broken by the sounds of footsteps on the stairwell.

They rushed to the doors but could already tell that it was the sound of humans, not the brutish and bulking creatures. Chandra leapt into view with her rifle at the ready but quickly lowered it as she identified Taylor.

"Good of you to join us," Taylor grinned.

"Sorry it took us as long as it did."

She looked over to see Eddie amongst the marines with a rifle in hand, and his ridiculous faded red bandana still about his head.

"Finally making a soldier of you, are we?" she asked.

"Don't get used to it. I fly for a living."

Taylor looked around and nodded in appreciation. Rains had blended into the unit so effectively and professionally that he'd forgotten the pilot was even with them. It never ceased to amaze him quite how good an asset the Lieutenant was. His appearance would never imply it.

A radio signal cut in with loud gunfire and shouts in the background.

"This is Parker. We're taking heavy fire in the parking garage, ground floor. Need immediate assistance!"

Taylor shot a glance to Chandra with a look of fear on his face.

"Go! Now!" shouted Chandra.

Taylor leapt to the stairs with his platoon close behind. He rushed down the stairs so quickly he almost fell flat on his face. As he took the final bend to the last stairwell, he leapt the last fifteen steps and landed hard at the base. The ceramic floor cracked under his feet. He got out of the stairway to find Captain Fournier ushering people out of the building.

"Captain! The garage, where is it?"

Fournier turned with a look of shock to see the concern in Taylor's face. He froze for just a moment before answering.

"South west corner, follow this..."

Before the Captain could continue, Taylor turned and sprinted away in the direction of the garage. He rushed so fast that the double automatic doors in front of him didn't have time to fully open. The shoulders of his armour made contact, tearing them from the frame. Taylor didn't even break stride as the others ran over the smashed doors.

The gunfire was growing louder, and he knew they were coming up on the fight. He reached a side door and could see into the garage through a small window. Parker and her unit were hunkered down around several police cruisers that were in a state of repair. Pulses were flashing across their positions, and they were rarely able to safely get any shots in return.

He looked towards the enemy positions and saw a dozen Mechs dug in, defending what appeared to be a large storage container that was definitely not human. Taylor didn't give it any more thought. He was only concerned with getting to the aid of Eli. He turned and looked down the corridor for another entrance, quickly leaping into action to find one. They rushed thirty metres down the corridor, but there was not a single entrance.

"God damn it, how the fuck do we get in?"

"Sir, I saw another entrance on the far side, but it was barricaded up. Only other way in is the doors to the road, but we'll have a hard time getting them open from the outside," Lam said.

He turned and looked in despair for any other options.

"Sir, this wall ain't too strong. It worked last time."

He put his hand to the wall and thought.

"Alright, but I don't want to give them any idea we're coming. What charges have we got left?"

Silva rushed up to their position and overheard the last of what they had said.

"We've still got two breaching charges. They'll take this baby down, no problem."

"Do it," said Taylor.

Silva turned and pointed to two of his team members to come forward. They drew out satchel charges and ripped off the tabs on the rear of the charges that revealed a self-adhesive surface. They slapped them onto the wall and pressed just a few buttons before turning to the Major.

"Twenty seconds, Sir."

"Clear out, take cover!" he ordered.

He rushed ten metres back and ducked his head down. He stared at his watch, counting the seconds. The satchel charges blew with a surprisingly quiet eruption that was a perfectly controlled charge, removing a segment from the interior wall wide enough for three marines to fit through.

"Go!" he shouted.

Lam was through the breach before Mitch could get back onto his feet. He was moved by his companion's faultless bravery. They were as eager to take on the Mechs as he was. He couldn't tell if they were rushing to the relief of friends or just wanting to feed their bloodlust, but it didn't matter.

As he got through the breach, a pulse rushed past him, killing the marine beside him. He had no idea who it had been. Mitch continued onwards while firing to the cover of a workstation. He hunkered down and pulled out his last grenade, launching it over to the enemy positions. Before it had landed, he was back on his feet and firing like hell. He watched in joy as the creatures were pelted with dozens of rounds before the grenade erupted amongst them.

He ducked back down to change his magazine to see Chandra rushing through the breach to join him. Gunfire raged from Parker's side of the room, and Taylor leapt to his feet to join in. Seeing the enemy taking continuous fire before them, and ducking for cover, he jumped over the desk.

"Taylor!" screamed Chandra.

It was too late to stop him. Mitch rushed at the enemy positions and jumped up onto the roof of a police cruiser that formed part of the enemy defences. He was stood tall above the last surviving creatures and quickly pointed his rifle, opening up on full auto. The others watched in amazement Taylor fired down into their positions. Chandra's face turned from concern to a hopeless grimace as she watched the morbid scene.

Taylor dropped the magazine onto the roof of the car and drew out another while he still stood on the roof.

"That's enough!" Chandra shouted to him.

He snapped around and glared at the Major. For a moment, he was in such a frenzied state he'd forgotten the friend she was to him. He took a deep breath and calmed himself. Taylor turned back to the carnage below and looked at the wash of blue blood seeping across the hard floor. Then the reason they had gotten there sprung back into his memory, and he turned and jumped from the roof. He rushed to Parker's position to find her sat beside the body of a dead marine.

"You okay?" he asked.

She looked up with sad eyes. Two tears seeped down her face. Chandra paced up to them and placed a hand on Taylor's shoulder. She looked down at Parker and the body of the marine beside her, but she knew there was nothing she could say to help, besides taking her mind off the loss.

"Any idea what's in that container?" asked Chandra. "Clearly it was important to them."

"No idea, but it had better be worth it."

Chandra nodded in agreement. She turned and hauled Taylor with her to investigate. As they reached the breach, a soldier stumbled through in pain, struggling to breathe. It was Williams, who Taylor had seen left for dead in the stairway.

"Still with us, then?"

Williams looked up with a pained expression and replied in a hoarse voice.

"Just about."

The two officers continued onwards to the container. It was ten metres long and five metres wide by five metres high.

"How on earth did that even get here?" she asked.

"And why?"

Jones and Fournier stepped up beside them as they stopped beside the curious container.

"Everyone from the bunker safe and secure?" asked Chandra.

"Yes," replied Fournier but was distracted by the sight of the container. They could see dents and gashes in the outer frame that could not have been caused by the firefight.

"Looks like that came down with a bird!"

They turned to see Eddie Rains approaching. They turned back, realising what he was saying made sense.

"Must have been shot down towards the end of the war," he continued.

"Yes, I have a report of a crash site just half a kilometre from here," replied Fournier.

"What the hell's in it?" asked Rains.

Taylor shrugged his shoulders.

"Let's find out," replied Chandra.

"Should we not leave it sealed and notify our commanders?" asked Fournier.

"Yes, after we've got an idea of what we're dealing with," she said.

Chandra stepped forward to what were clearly the entrance doors and studied the locking mechanism for just a moment. It had two levers to release the catches but no security device of any kind. She lifted each lever, and the door seal burst open. The doors themselves only opened a few centimetres. She squeezed her finger through the gaps and heaved them open.

"My God," said Taylor.

They stood before twenty incubation chambers like those they had seen in Paris, during the raid. But these containers were not empty, as they had found the others after the war. The humans, or what appeared to be humans, were still inside. A power source in the centre of the container was connected to them all. Two of the chambers were damaged and had clearly lost power, but the rest were completely intact.

"What is this?" asked Fournier.

"A piece of the puzzle which could be vital to our future," replied Chandra.

She turned to Silva. "Sergeant, contact Commander

Phillips. I want an immediate evac of this freighter to Ramstein."

"Yes, Ma'am, what shall I say are the contents?"

"You don't tell them anything. All they need to know is the weight and size for transport. Nobody knows about this until it's in safe hands. She turned to Taylor.

"Get hold of Captain Reyes. He's still working as a liaison officer in Ramstein. We can trust him with this, so he can liaise with Phillips to sort this out."

"Why the secrecy?" asked Jones.

"Because we have no idea what we are dealing with here. Back in Paris, we saw hundreds of thousands of these chambers. We need to know what their purpose is, and what is inside. We have no idea if these are human prisoners, clones, or re-education and indoctrination modules. We only trust those we know with this for now."

She turned back to the rest of the troops in the room.

"You are all sworn to secrecy in what you see here today. It is not to be discussed again, even amongst yourselves. This could be a major breakthrough for humanity in our struggle against the enemy. Let's make sure it gets to Ramstein safely."

CHAPTER SEVEN

The troops of Inter-Allied sat in a temporary dining shelter enjoying their evening meal. Through the windows of the solid structure they could see the snow growing ever thicker, but the warm heaters kept them grateful they were not out in it. Taylor sat with Chandra and Parker either side of him and the rest the officers and senior NCOs of the Company.

"I hear we're being reinforced soon," said Silva.

Chandra smiled. "And where would you hear such a thing, Sergeant?"

"You know, here and there."

"More scuttlebutt?"

"I'd say by your reaction that the Sergeant is on the ball," Taylor grinned.

She nodded in agreement.

"That's certainly the plan, and God knows we need it."

The table fell quiet as they all thought about what that might mean.

"Surely it's time our tour of duty was over and someone else took over our job?" asked Taylor.

"Well, I'd say France is clearing up of any remaining insurgency pretty quickly, thanks to our efforts. Construction and building is already well underway, and this country is starting to get back on its feet."

"Then why do we need reinforcing at this stage?"

"The next phase of the war is coming. We all knew it would. While the Krycenaeans occupy the Moon, or any territory in this solar system, there can be no peace."

The table went quiet once again. Chandra had accepted long ago that the war was not over, but the others had hoped for it. Jones finally spoke up.

"This war has almost killed me many times over. I have been through hell and given everything I have. That isn't to diminish the rest of your service and devotion. But I, for one, am finished. Is there not a point where a man has simply done enough? Have we not all done enough for a lifetime?"

The others remained silent. They were stunned by the Captain's words. He was as respected in the Company as much as the two Majors, and they all knew his word had both merit and influence. Chandra didn't agree, but she found it hard to speak up against him. She finally tried to speak but was interrupted by Taylor.

"I agree. Are we to continue until every last one of us is dead? What purpose would that serve? How can we ask the men and women of this Company to go on, knowing that there is no light at the end of the tunnel, and nothing to work towards, nothing to go home to?"

"It isn't an ideal situation, or one I would ever have wished on any of us. But simply put, we are an essential part of the line that holds the defences of this world together. If it were not us out here, enduring such hardships, who would it be? Would you leave civilians to their deaths, rather than face the enemy yourselves?"

"But when do you draw the line?" asked Jones. "Historically wars go on and on. New reasons, new enemies, and the same soldiers can't keep fighting them day after day, year after year."

Chandra took a deep breath, sighing as she realised the morale of the Company was being sapped away. None of the others spoke. She could see they were all thinking hard about Jones' words, and there wasn't one among them who didn't agree with him.

"These past few months we have fought over ground which saw some of the greatest and most bloodthirsty battles the world's ever known. You all know your history. Look back to the twentieth century when a relentless enemy sought to conquer the world."

She took a deep breath again as they thought back to their military history.

"When Hitler took hold of Europe, Britain was all that stood against the Nazi regime. Surrounded on all sides, it was a state of total war. Negotiation and diplomacy was at its end. That war would end when one side was utterly vanquished. Our troops did not get leave. Their leave would be when victory was won, and the war was over."

She could see they thought about her lesson in history, but it had not yet changed their minds.

"Did the allies stop when France was re-taken, with an enemy still on the doorstep? No. They knew that peace could only be won through absolute victory. Make no mistake. This war is not over. You can go back to your homes and try and enjoy a normal life until the next invasion, or you can take the fight to the enemy with me."

Taylor looked up and began to realise what her initial words had meant.

"We're going to the Moon, aren't we? It's the only reason we'd be reinforced so quickly after the war was over. We're invading the Moon."

She shook her head, knowing that her privileged information was out.

"Keep your voice down," she said.

Jones sighed in disbelief as she continued on at a whisper.

"Yes. The Moon must be re-taken. This unit has more experience against the enemy than any other. It has proven its worth, and Taylor's marines have already fought there before. We're going to the Moon, and we're ridding ourselves of this invading force for good!"

The rest of the evening was a quiet and sombre affair as all who had sat at that table thought of the perils that were to come. They watched the rest of the Company joyfully party, but they could think of nothing else. Taylor and Parker went to bed that night and lay beside each other in silence. It was a sadness they had wished they'd never feel again.

* * *

"Major Taylor! Major Taylor!"

Mitch awoke at the sound of his voice being bellowed out by Silva. The Sergeant continued to bark his name, and it was getting louder as he closed the distance to his billet. Eli had arisen at the noise and was groaning at being woken so harshly. They could tell from the natural light flooding through the partially transparent fabric of the field billet that the sun had recently risen to bring them into the next day.

"Major Taylor!"

The calls continued. He could tell that it was urgent, and by the concern in Silva's harsh voice, he could already tell that it was not going to be good news. He leapt from his bed and pulled on his boots and coat. He still war his BDUs from the night before. The heaters they had kept the billets from freezing, but it was far from warm. He opened the door to find Silva just reaching him. He could see a distraught look in the man's eyes. He'd rarely seen such fear from the steadfast Sergeant.

"What is it?"

"Sir, you need to come with me, now!"

Taylor leapt out of the billet and followed the Sergeant. He'd never have taken orders from any NCO, but it was clear to him that he needed to trust Silva. The Sergeant led him to Commander Phillips' command vehicle and stepped inside with him. Phillips and Chandra were stood around the briefing table, and Jones entered shortly after.

"What the hell's going on?" insisted Taylor.

"I have just had official confirmation that thirty minutes ago, there was an attack at Ramstein air base."

"What? How?"

"Preliminary reports suggest that an overwhelming force of enemy aircraft entered the atmosphere at speed and carried out a lightning fast attack which flattened most of the base. They struck quickly before any intercept fighters could counter them."

"What about the ground defences?" Taylor asked.

"Seems they took down a few of the enemy bombers, but much of the system had still not been repaired since the last battle there. The base was only just getting operational again."

"Christ," whispered Jones.

"What are the casualties?"

"The only contact we have had is with the crew of the Deveron who narrowly escaped the same fate as they were on the way back from a refit in England, but their Captain, Reyes, was on the base when the attack struck. So we must assume he is among the dead."

Taylor shook his head in disbelief. Then he remembered Chandra sending their last find to the research facilities there.

"The incubation chambers?"

"The only reports we have back so far are from the Deveron, and it doesn't look good. These are the initial images they sent."

Phillips tapped a few keys on the glass display of the table, and it lit up with the images of the devastated base. As a US base, it had been quickly rebuilt after it had been re-captured from the enemy. It was seen as vital to morale to rebuild what had become such a symbol of hope for them all. Now it lay in ruins once again. Fire and smoke rose from the wasteland the base had become. They could just make out parts of raptors and other aircraft that had been scattered amongst the debris.

"How many personnel were in Ramstein?"

"The US deployment was about fifteen thousand, with maybe another ten thousand foreign troops and civilians."

Taylor gasped at the news.

"Reyes was a good man, one of many," he replied.

"Why now?" asked Jones. "Why Ramstein? I thought the war on Earth was over?"

"Clearly not," replied Phillips.

"It is too much of a coincidence that the only attack they have launched since their retreat was against the base where we sent the only remaining incubation chambers we have found so far," stated Chandra.

"You believe they are that valuable to them?" asked Jones.

"I believe whatever we would have learnt from them was worth everything to the enemy," she replied.

"This confirms one thing for certain," replied Phillips. "This war isn't over."

Taylor could feel the anger growing inside him. He thought of his comments the night before, how he'd wanted it all to end. Now he remembered why they continued fighting.

"Reyes was a good friend and a great officer. I will not stand by and let this attack go unanswered."

Chandra nodded in agreement. She was glad of having his support back but hated the circumstances that had led to it. Mitch looked to Jones who was still staring at the images of the devastated base.

"Jones, I know what we said before. But times have changed. We're in this fight whether we like it or not. Will you stand by us?"

He looked up with a fierce anger that Taylor had not

seen since the enemy had retreated from Earth. Gone was the peace in his eyes.

"I want every one of those bastards dead. I will not stand by to see our people suffer any longer against these animals!"

Chandra could see the Captain was almost reduced to tears. He, more than any of them, had suffered the most against the invaders, and she knew it was a horrible thing to ask him to face them time and time again.

"I want this news kept on the QT for now. It could destroy morale among our armies," ordered Phillips.

Before any of the others had time to speak, they heard cries ring out around the base. They rushed to the door of the command vehicle to look out across the square in Reims that had become their staging ground. Troops were shouting as they ran towards a large display screen in the opposite end of the square. Even from the distance, Taylor could just make out scenes of devastation on the screen as hundreds of troops flocked to it. Phillips rushed to the edge of the ramp and shouted out to the nearest passing soldier. They were rushing towards the screen in a frenzy.

"Private! What's going on?" he asked.

"They've bombed Ramstein! The fuckers have bombed Ramstein!"

Phillips turned and shook his head in disbelief.

"Guess it's a little late," said Chandra.

They turned to see a news anchor appear on the screen overlaid on top of the aerial images of the burning ruins.

"I've seen enough," whispered Taylor.

He jumped from the ramp as the others watched the anger build among the troops. Phillips smiled as he realised their morale wasn't dead. They weren't at a loss. They were angry, and they wanted blood. Taylor strode away from the scene. Only Silva saw him leave and rushed after him.

"Where are you going, Sir?" he insisted.

"We are at war, Sergeant. I am going to make sure we have what we need to win it."

"Mind if I tag along?"

He turned and saw the Sergeant was eager to assist.

"Sure."

They continued on to the landing ground where the Company's copters had been based. Kato and Rains were taking delivery of some components beside the last intact vehicle they had between them.

"Major! What's the ruckus all about?" asked Rains.

Taylor responded in a grim tone. "Ramstein, it's gone."

"What are you talking about, man?"

"Bombed to hell this morning."

"Fuck," he replied. "What are you doing here?"

"I need a ride, to Paris."

"Well, sure, you got mission clearance?"

"You just got it from me."

Rains smiled. He knew just like many times before that

it was best not to ask.

"Let's fire this bird up."

* * *

Taylor rushed into the HQ in Paris. It was a freshly built administrative quarters in the centre of the city that General Schulz was using as his command post during the reconstruction. Despite being a foreign officer, his reputation and achievements had awarded him an honorary rank within France and much support among its people. Taylor's ID got him through the gate security and into the building, but the General's secretary tried to stop him. She was a well-kept civilian in a perfectly cut and clean suit.

"Sir, you can't see the General without an appointment."

He continued on at a brisk pace that she could do nothing to stop. Taylor burst through the doors to the General's office with Silva close behind. Schulz looked up and smiled at the sight of the Major. Several other officers and the city Mayor sat around a table with him.

"Major Taylor, it is an honour to have such a decorated officer among us."

He looked to his secretary who was flustered. "It's okay, leave us."

"Cut the bullshit, General. Ramstein has been flattened. This war is very much back on."

"I am aware of that fact, Major."

"The Moon must be taken back, and I want in!"

"Your enthusiasm and determination is to be admired, Major."

"General. We have what it takes. I know the colony, and we have one of the finest combat units in the world. But this war has taken a heavy toll. We need troops, guns, and we need to be brought back up to strength. Not a few dozen to fulfil a company. We need a battalion once again."

Schulz took a deep breath and looked across at his advisers. One of them finally spoke up, a French officer.

"Sir, the Immortals leading the charge could give an immense boost to morale."

Schulz nodded. Taylor could see that the General felt no ill will towards him, and he was starting to understand it. They each had their part to play and needed each other.

"You would choose to remain under my command?" asked Schulz.

"I believe you'll be placed in charge of any Moon deployment, Sir. I want to be where the action is."

"Your Company is an amalgamation of British and American troops, is it not?"

"Yes, Sir."

"Then it is only fitting that we maintain that. I will get you the troops and equipment you need, if you agree to be the spearhead of my operation. The troops need heroes, Major, and you're a poster boy that can turn the tide in the coming battles."

Taylor nodded. "It would be an honour, Sir."

"Return to your people. I'll have what you need sorted within the next twenty-four hours."

Silva's eyes widened. He'd never seen any change be made so rapidly in his long time of service. Taylor turned and strode out of the room. Silva was close by his side.

"Will he do it? Really get you everything you have asked for?"

"Yes, because we're an asset to him that he can't afford to lose. Much more fighting, and there'll be nothing left of the Immortals."

"Sir, if you don't mind me asking. Yesterday, you wanted to put down your rifle and see an end to the fighting. Now you want to be at the forefront of a second war?"

"It's not a new war. The old one just never ended. I see that now. Chandra was right all along. She could see that and I couldn't. This war will end when one race is utterly destroyed."

Silva shook his head in astonishment, but he was glad to see Taylor back to his old self. They rushed back to the copter to find Rains and Kato waiting on the ramp, each with a coffee in hand.

"You get what you were after?" asked Eddie.

"Hell, yes. We're going back to war, Lieutenant. Are you ready to return to the Moon?"

"Fuck, yes. All those missions I flew to get aid up there.

Pissed me off when we lost the colony for good. We going to take it to the bastards?"

"That's the plan."

"Alright!"

He threw out the contents of the coffee onto the roadside and rushed into the copter to take them back to Reims. When they got back to the city, they found Chandra and Jones waiting for them at the landing zone. They were stood in thick coats beside a heater the pilots had set up for working on the copters. As soon as they had landed, Taylor was out the door and heading down the ramp to pass on the news.

"Taylor, I've just heard from Field Marshal Copley himself. He says you've been causing quite a stir, and that we're getting fresh troops tomorrow morning."

"It was time we got back up to strength," he replied.

She smiled. "How many toes did you tread on to get this?"

"Only a few. The only proviso is that we spearhead the Moon assault, that okay with you?"

"It's what I've been God damn telling you these past few weeks, isn't it?"

"So you aren't pissed that I went over you on this?"

"Major, getting us the support we need is not going over my head! Good work, let's just see what they send us."

The evening was a strange mix of sombre reflection on

what they had lost in Ramstein, and in what excitement lay ahead. They had all built such a hatred for the enemy that to put their lives on the line no longer mattered. It was clear to them all now what must be done. Chandra tapped her glass and drew the room to silence.

"We lost a great many friends and comrades today. They were not the first and will not be the last. Remember them, for they are the reason we are still alive today. To our fallen friends!"

She lifted her glass to an enthusiastic cheer. She turned to Taylor who sat alone with a glass of beer, staring into the distance in a world of his own.

"You asked when this war would be over for us?" she asked.

Taylor snapped out of it and turned to her with a look of curiosity of what wisdom she might impart.

"It'll be over for us when it's over for the world."

He smiled.

"What?" she asked.

"Yesterday, that would have just pissed me off."

"And now?"

"Now I wonder what any of our lives are really for. Yesterday, I wanted to end this life of soldering, but what would I do? What else are people like us made for?"

"Christ. You're not going to go all philosophical on me, are you? I'll go and find the chaplain if this is to continue."

"You must give it some thought from time to time?"

"Sure, and my conclusion is I am glad I have a purpose in life. I see people wasting away doing nothing, achieving nothing. I never wanted fame or fortune, but to know that I'm doing something good with my life, that's enough. Look at you, all that and a damn statue!"

Taylor chuckled. "Hey, I never wanted that shit."

"But it's there all the same, and not for no good reason."

She could see she'd got back the officer she had come to admire so much. It warmed her to know she kept his company in such hard times.

* * *

Morning came and the Company formed up at a former playing field of a school that had been allocated to the fresh troops that were arriving. It was almost 0900 hours, and they stood calmly in the cold.

"You really believe anyone is coming?" asked Jones.

"From the hassle Taylor whipped up yesterday, yeah I believe so."

Seconds later, they heard the roar of engines as copters tore across the sky towards them. Eddie and Kato sat on a wall beside the Company in a relaxed manner. They wanted to see what fresh equipment was coming with their own eyes. The two pilots leapt to their feet as they heard the familiar sound of the modified engines they'd grafted to their own copters. Then they came into view.

"What the fuck is that?" asked Eddie.

"Nothing we've seen before."

Five aircraft burst into view that were bigger than the Eagle copters they had used previously, but they seemed to move with the same speed and nimble manoeuvrability. They descended quickly and landed down on the green in front of them. The fast decent and engines blasted a snowdrift across the fields, splashing the awaiting Company with a spray of white powder.

The ramps slammed down, and troops poured out from the craft, each equipped with Reitech's finest. As the NCOs formed up the troops, a Captain strode forward to greet them. He saluted as he got with a few metres but continued onwards to shake the hand of Chandra and then the others.

"Captain Jackson, 15th Marine Expeditionary Unit."

Taylor looked at the Captain's pristine new equipment and those of his troops. Jackson caught a glimpse of Taylor's surprise at their attire.

"Don't let the flashy new gear fool you, Major. These boys have been in the fight since day one and the shit hit the fan. Since the war ended, we have been refitting and re-equipping for our next deployment."

"What are your orders, Captain?" asked Chandra.

"I have three hundred marines at my command. I have been ordered to place these troops and myself under your command in the formation of an Inter-Allied Battalion,

Ma'am."

She smiled in response. "Bloody hell."

Chandra turned to Taylor in surprise. "You really did it."

"It's an honour to be here, Ma'am. You've all become legends back home."

She went to respond when they were interrupted by more aircraft approaching. They turned to see another five of the unique craft roar overhead and bank hard to come in to land beside the others.

"They with you?" she asked.

"No, Ma'am, I was informed there would be British troops joining us at this LZ."

She turned in surprise to see the craft descend and land behind the formed up marines."

The ramps slammed down into the snow and British soldiers poured from the doors to form up beside their American counterparts.

"How is this possible?" asked Chandra.

"You asked for your support, you got it," replied Jackson.

She looked at him with a puzzled expression.

"And when in your time in service have you ever got what you asked for?"

The engines of the craft powered down as the hundreds of British soldiers formed up before them. Chandra and Taylor noticed the sound of a vehicle approaching and turned to see Phillips' jeep heading for them. She ordered the troops to attention as he jumped from the vehicle as it came to a halt.

"Major Chandra, Major Taylor. Your reinforcements as requested."

The British officer leading the newly arrived troops strode up to them and saluted.

"Lieutenant Grey, 2nd Parachute Regiment."

Taylor looked up at the man with a puzzled expression. He was twenty years older than Mitch would have expected for a Lieutenant. The man was short but strongly built. He looked like he'd served for decades as a soldier.

"You have what, two Companies there, and you are in charge?"

"My apologies, Sir. Most of our officers were killed when our HQ was hit a few weeks back. I am the senior officer at present."

"You don't have to apologise, Lieutenant. Your presence is much appreciated."

The Commander interrupted before Taylor could speak.

"I am glad to see you have all now met. General Schulz caused quite a stir on both sides of the pond and managed to assemble quite the force for you. General White and Field Marshal Copley discussed this personally and agreed to send you some of the best veteran infantry they had to offer. At last look, you have around three hundred from 15th Marine Expeditionary, and four hundred from the Parachute Regiment, including fifty US rangers who fought with them during the war. All have substantial combat experience and will serve you well.

"Sir, if I might add. We saw plenty of combat through this war, as I am sure Lieutenant Grey has, but all the troops under my command have been amazed by what you, The Immortals, have achieved. To join you is a dream they could never have imagined," Captain Jackson said.

Phillips interrupted once again.

"Excuse me, Gentlemen, but I have pressing matters to attend to. I must relay a few more points before I leave. All that you see here is to be amalgamated into the 2nd Inter-Allied Battalion, and will come under the new 7th Army under the command of General Schulz. It is a joint taskforce from around the world, with American, British and German troops forming the core. Inter-Allied will come under the command of the newly appointed Colonel Chandra."

She looked up in shock at the title. She had briefly held the rank as a temporary status, but the thought of the promotion had long since passed.

"I am sorry this promotion could not be done more formally, but there are more pressing matters to deal with. As Battalion Commander, you are to organise the Companies as you see fit, and promote as necessary to make this Battalion fully combat ready. Be sure that you are ready to move out in three days. Good luck, Colonel."

Phillips reached out his hand to shake Chandra's. She was left speechless as he turned and left. She peered out at the eight hundred troops she now commanded in astonishment. They all wore a new camouflage pattern that had become an Allied standard and made them look scruffy by comparison. Taylor leant in and whispered to her.

"They are awaiting a speech."

She nodded as she snapped out of the daze and stepped forward. She coughed and cleared her throat, finally finding her words.

"Welcome to Reims, and the 2nd Inter-Allied Battalion! During the last year, we have fought over these lands as if they were our own. The divide between countries and nationalities is over. We stand now as humans, united against a common enemy. I know you have all seen your fair share of combat in this bloody war, but that was just the beginning."

She stepped forward and walked along the row of troops that were twenty ranks deep. She bellowed at the top of her voice, so she could just about be heard in all corners.

"We started this war ill prepared. We didn't have the experience, the weapons. We blundered through until our sheer stubbornness, adaptability, and our heroism got us through. That time is over. We have the equipment, the support, and the knowledge. In the coming days, we will leave this planet to take the fight to the enemy."

She paused for a second to get her breath back.

"There are no green troops here today, only combat hardened veterans. Today is not for training. Inter-Allied is a family, and we have a bond that makes us unbreakable. Tomorrow we begin training as a battalion, but today your mission is to make that bond with each other. Get your billets in order, settle in, but most importantly, get to know those who will alongside you. Welcome to the Immortals!"

Cheers rang out across the Battalion, sending a shiver down her spine. It was a level of excitement she had not heard in a long time. For so long she had seen their number dwindle, and she never thought she'd see the day that they were once again a formidable force.

"That'll be all. Fall out!"

Ecstatic cheers rang out once again as the NCOs relayed the command, the columns split apart, and the troops mixed.

"That was quite a speech," exclaimed Taylor.

"I hope so. I never thought to plan anything. If I am completely honest, I was sceptical that anyone would turn up," she replied.

"No faith," he jested.

"In you, yes, but in those who made you promises, not so much."

Lieutenant Grey signalled for several of his soldiers to carry over crates that they were unloading from the copters. They lugged the boxes as the other officers still stood marvelling on the foray of shiny new equipment.

"Colonel Chandra, I was instructed to deliver this equipment to you. The latest uniforms for the whole of your Company here."

She looked at the Lieutenant in shock, never before had they been given such priority. She turned to Taylor.

"You really did kick over more than a few stones, Major. Sergeant Silva, I will leave the distribution of this equipment in your hands."

She looked out at the shabby Company she had led through the worst of it. They wore a ragged mix of overcoats that had been acquired in any way possible from any service or civilian source. Many of their uniforms were ripped and patched over with ingrained blood and dust that was immovable.

"It'll do the troops a lot of good. We've been a ramshackle mix since we were first merged."

Another officer rushed up to Jackson's side and stopped to salute the Colonel. The woman was of Asian descent and stood surprisingly tall beside the Captain.

"Colonel Chandra," stated Jackson. "This is Lieutenant Ota, my second in command."

"Welcome, Lieutenant."

"Thank you, Ma'am."

"I want all senior NCOs and officers to join me at the mess. Follow me," ordered Chandra.

It wasn't long before the group were enthralled in conversation around the same table they had sat arguing whether or not to continue fighting, only two days before. Chandra could see that new life had been breathed into the troops. More so than anything, she was grateful to have Taylor back on her side.

"Lieutenant Grey, you said the officers of your Company were killed in one unlucky attack, how did you survive?"

Grey sat up tall. She could tell he was an immensely proud man, but curiosity required her to know his story.

"My CO and all the officers of the Company were in a briefing with the Colonel of our Battalion and many other officers. It was an emergency meeting called in the field. Their command vehicle was struck by enemy artillery, just bad luck I am afraid. As for how I escaped that fate, I was not an officer but CSM at the time. I was promoted in the field after the attack."

"Company Sergeant Major to Lieutenant? Got to be a kick in the balls?" asked Jones.

"It's certainly been a challenge, Sir," he replied.

Jones chuckled. "Amongst us at this table, you don't need to call anyone Sir."

"Are you happy in your new role, Lieutenant?" asked Chandra.

"Honestly, Ma'am?"

"Speak freely here."

"I would never have chosen it, but I will continue to do what is required of me. I didn't sign up to the Army thinking I could have my own way."

Chandra laughed.

"Well, Lieutenant, you'll fit in here just fine."

CHAPTER EIGHT

It was a new day and a seemingly new dawn for Inter-Allied. Chandra and Taylor stood before eight hundred of the finest soldiers Earth had to offer, and they were theirs to do with as they saw fit.

"Hell of a sight, ain't it?" asked Taylor.

"Damn right," Chandra whispered in reply.

She watched as the NCOs make their inspections.

"You know I heard Reiter wasn't in Ramstein. He's still alive," Taylor went on.

"Bloody hell, the crazy bastard's still with us. Good, we'll need him."

They were formed up on the hard standing of the old school. It had been abandoned for so many months that it was beginning to look derelict. The troops fell quiet as the NCOs took up their positions and awaited the Colonel.

"Good morning to you all!" she called. "You all have

come from proud units, just as we had. Inter-Allied started as a simple way to combine two key units during the battle for France. As time went on, more were added, to the extent that you could no longer begin to explain our identity. I do not ask you to forget where you came from but to embrace where you are now. We stand together as one!"

A cheer rang out as the NCOs led the call.

"No soldier likes re-organisation. We get used to what we have. I will do my very best to change as little as humanly possible. From now on, the Battalion will be structured as four Companies. Major Taylor will remain second in command for Inter-Allied. Alpha Company will be commanded by Captain Jones and will encompass the remaining members of my old Company, with a number drawn from 2 Para to bring them up to strength."

She paced along the line and looked to the officers to see Jones nod in gratitude.

"Bravo Company, the remainder of 2 para, will be under the command of Lieutenant Grey. Charlie and Delta are to be led by Captain Jackson and Lieutenant Ota respectively. The US rangers among you are to report to the Charlie and Delta to make up their number."

She took in a deep breath and looked across at the troops' faces. They seemed content with the news.

"Lastly, I am appointing Sergeant Silva to Company Sergeant Major. He has been a force of reason and discipline throughout this war, and I cannot think of a better soldier to keep things in order. Congratulations Sergeant!"

Whistles broke the silence, and the troops that had been with them since the beginning clapped to the Sergeant's success. She smiled at their appreciation. Silva was humbled and could not bring himself to discipline them for such open support. Chandra lifted up her hand to request silence, and it was quickly given.

"Company commanders have been sent full lists of those personnel who will serve under them. Please report to them upon dismissal. We're lacking the NCOs and officers we need at platoon level, and I will leave that to Company commanders to resolve as they see fit. You will see along the back wall there four letters. Those are the designated assembly areas for each Company."

She could see a number of the troops start to shiver in the cool morning breeze.

"It is vital that this Battalion learns to work as one in the shortest time possible. Change is never easy, and I know that you will all have become closely tied with those you have served beside. That same bond must now be extended to all standing here today. Thank you. Fall out and assemble with your Company leaders.

She nodded to Silva to relay her commands. Within seconds, the troops were scattering to assemble as requested. Most of the officers rushed to take command of their troops, but Taylor watched in amazement.

"Strange isn't it?" asked Chandra.

"What's that?"

"To be stood back here watching while everything is done for you."

"For now, but we won't be taking desk jobs anytime soon."

"True. Although at Battalion HQ we will need some additional staff. Having Silva at hand will be most useful to us, but we are still lacking a medical officer, quartermaster and several other administrative staff. A chaplain may also be useful."

"Really? For what?"

"The pressure these troops are under on a daily basis, don't you think they could do with some outlet?"

Taylor shook his head.

"Not much of a believer myself."

"You don't have to believe in anything to simply just have someone to talk to. I don't want any cracks appearing in this Battalion, so whatever is necessary to keep it strong will be done."

They watched as the four Company commanders quickly formed up their troops, and it was clear the Battalion was quickly taking shape. Chandra marvelled at the troops who now all wore matching uniforms for the first time since amalgamation.

"We are finally getting the army we always needed," she

stated.

"We need to put these troops through combat simulations. We need to know they are going to be able to work together as sharply as the Company always has done."

"Agreed. Sergeant Major!" she yelled.

Silva rushed to her position.

"Sergeant, I am placing you in charge of assembling a series of combat tests. You have free rein to use the former industrial park a kilometre south of here for any and all exercises, including live fire. Put them through their paces."

"Yes Ma'am!"

He rushed off with a new level of enthusiasm.

"Schulz may have give us all this, but he's going to expect a lot in return," she whispered.

"Agreed, but wouldn't it be expected, anyway?"

She nodded in agreement. It seemed hard to imagine that they could have ever played a larger part in the war.

"Shouldn't we get in on this training?" asked Taylor.

"Not yet, this is our Battalion now. Let the troops get used to the chain of command. Right now we have other work ahead of us. We may have wings, but we'll need more substantial transport for where we're going."

"Surely not our problem to sort out?"

"Maybe so, but I'd rather have the pick of it before we get dumped on some civilian liner and sent up into enemy territory. Phillips promised me he'd sort it, and I want to make sure he has kept his word. Follow me."

Half an hour later they stood at their former landing zone in Reims. Rains and Kato were desperately trying to salvage parts from the wreckage they had recovered to use as a donor for the last copter. Rains noticed them approaching and spoke out as he continued to use a power wrench.

"Shame you couldn't get us some of those shiny new rides."

Chandra smiled as they heard a large ship approaching their positions.

They looked up to the sky to see an Achilles class vessel roar into view and come in to land. It was large enough to almost completely fill the landing zone from where they had been operational.

"You might be careful what you wish for," replied Chandra.

The vessel descended to the ground, and Taylor could make out the name, Deveron.

"Reyes' ship, what's it doing here?" he asked.

A ramp lowered from the vessel, and an officer stepped out to greet them. Taylor had seen him before but had never shared words.

"Lieutenant Ryan at your service."

"Welcome to Reims, Lieutenant," replied Chandra.

"I am sorry to hear of the loss of your Captain, he was

a good man," Taylor added.

"Thank you, Sir."

"Major, the Deveron has been assigned to our Battalion as long range transport for the foreseeable future, along with three other Achilles class frigates."

Taylor stepped around the Lieutenant and peered down the hull of the ship. He recognised the name, but much of the rest was new to him.

"Some refit, hey, Lieutenant?"

"Yes, Sir, we've been given new engines, new weapons, things I've never seen in my life."

Eddie strolled up to their positions.

"Looks like someone has taken my improvements to a larger scale."

"Are you Lieutenant Rains?"

"One and only," he replied.

"We are carrying two new Eagle HVs which are to be delivered to you."

Eddie turned in shock as he raised an eyebrow in astonishment.

"Taylor, who's ass have you kissed to get us such treatment?"

Before they could marvel at the technology any further, a jeep drew up beside them. The driver leapt out within a second of it drawing to a halt.

"Colonel Chandra?" she asked.

"Yes."

"Orders from Commander Phillips, you and Major Taylor are to assemble at briefing shelter A at 1100 hours."

"Why did this not get relayed via comms?" she asked.

"The Commander asked me to relay the order personally, and for your ears only, Ma'am."

"Alright, thank you, you can be on your way."

As the jeep pulled away, she looked down at her watch to see there was little time before they were to be summoned.

"We were supposed to have another day," said Taylor.

"When does anything work to the schedule we need?" she responded. "Come on, I'm eager to see what is in store for us."

* * *

Chandra and Taylor stepped into the briefing shelter with just seconds to spare. Several dozen other officers awaited the Commander to start. They barely recognised anyone in the room. It was a stark reminder of how much they had lost in the war. A door towards the front of the room opened, and General Schulz stepped through with several of his staff. Nobody was even aware that he had arrived in the city, but they all understood it meant there was a matter of great importance.

"Welcome all of you. A new operation is about to begin which will see you all tested to your sheer limits. We drove the enemy from this planet, and yet we have not driven them from human territory. As long as the enemy remain on the Moon, humanity is in danger. Tomorrow we launch the greatest military operation outside of Earth boundaries that has ever taken place in human history."

Several gasps rang out. Taylor could see that there was a mix of officers from around the world, including several Americans.

"Schulz has been gathering forces here, and we didn't even know it," he whispered.

"It's as good a place as any," replied Chandra.

"I'd like to introduce you all to Commander Kelly, the former military leader of the Moon colony forces."

Schulz ushered the Commander up to take a seat beside him.

"The Commander's efforts in defending his colony and keeping his people safe are to be commended. It is only natural that he would want a stake in this new enterprise to free the lands he calls home."

The officers around the room clapped Kelly as he took to the stage beside the General. Schulz called quiet and tapped a few buttons before him which displayed their solar system behind him.

"If we are to fight a war outside of Earth's boundaries, we need a foothold in space, one which we no longer have. The L2 station is by far our best option. We know the enemy occupy the station but are unsure of their exact strength. Tomorrow you will depart for L2 and take it with a rapid strike before they can bolster their forces. It is vital that we gain this position in order to continue to the Lunar colony."

"I am hearing a lot of unknowns here," whispered Taylor.

"What do you expect? We lost everything outside of this atmosphere," replied Chandra.

"Between you all, you can field approximately six thousand troops and will make up the initial raid to take L2 in what is to be known as Operation Phoenix."

Chandra smiled.

"He's pretty confident of victory, then?" she whispered.

"I fucking hope so, or it'll be our asses left for dead up there," replied Taylor.

* * *

Taylor slumped into bed after a half day of planning for the operation. He was exhausted from seemingly doing nothing but sitting and listening. Just a few minutes after lying down alone, there was a knock on the door. He knew Parker wouldn't have stopped at the door.

"Come!" he called as he sat up.

To Taylor's surprise it was Commander Kelly who stepped through. He was alone, and it put Mitch's guard up. His hand instinctively closed towards his pistol, but he stopped short of taking the grip in hand.

"I didn't come to squabble, Major."

Taylor looked down at his hand held next to the pistol like an old gunslinger.

"You'll forgive me, Commander. Our last meeting was not a friendly one."

"Appreciated, and I want that resolved. Tomorrow we go to war together. Schulz may still be in command, but you will also be accountable to me. Will that be a problem?"

"Not unless you try and get me and mine killed."

"The General tells me that you volunteered for this offensive, is that correct?"

Taylor nodded.

"It means a lot. My soldiers believed you only interested in Earth. It will go a long way to mending fences with them to see you join our side."

"I was never not on your side, but I had my orders just like everyone else."

"And you always follow them?" he replied.

Taylor smiled. "I'm sorry we left you to fend for yourselves, and I am sorry we could not help further. What more do you want me to say?"

"Nothing, that is quite enough. You're a hero here on Earth, so take your place among us as the same. If you can be half the soldier you have been through this war, then we'd be foolish not to have you with us."

Taylor nodded in agreement.

"That'll be all. Good luck tomorrow, and thank you for

joining us."

"And to you, Sir. It will be an honour to serve with you."

* * *

"Good morning to you all!" shouted Chandra.

She stood before the Battalion formed up in front of the four Achilles frigates. Their assault copters were loaded, and everything was ready for their departure. The ground was quiet now as they all awaited the final order to depart.

"I would have greatly preferred to have many weeks to get this battalion in order. However, you are all experienced and more than competent soldiers. From now on, we are a family. It doesn't matter if you were here from the very start or joined yesterday! Today we embark on the only space based military assault in the history of our race, so let's do it right!"

She stopped as she listened to a message coming through on her intercom.

"This is it. We have been ordered to embark on Operation Phoenix. Load up and move out!"

There was no cheering or excitement amongst them. They all wanted to see an end to the enemy, but few wanted to engage them in combat again. The troops swarmed to the boats in silence. Chandra turned as she caught sight of a soldier approaching at her flank. It was Commander Kelly. His worn old uniform had been replaced by the same new camouflage patterns; something that kept them uniformed even if the pattern served no purpose where they were going. Despite his clean new gear, the same grizzled veteran lay beneath.

"Glad to have you with us, Colonel!" he shouted, approaching with his hand forward to shake hers.

"Sir, it's an honour to be a part of this enterprise. I know there is still ill will towards some of my Battalion for their service on your colony at the start of this war. I pray that now that can be put to rest when we strive forward together."

Kelly looked over and nodded to Taylor.

"I think we have put that to rest, Colonel. There's no time or energy left to worry about what has been. We want our colony back, and anyone who is willing to assist us to that end will be eternally our friend. L2 will be a major stepping stone to getting our homes back. I wish you every luck."

"And to you, Sir," replied Chandra.

She turned and followed Taylor to the frigates awaiting them. They boarded the Deveron together, and Taylor felt a tingle run down his spine as he stepped aboard once again. It was a stark reminder of their last visit to the Moon which had been his first experience of the harrowing enemy. He thought back to Reyes and was glad to see the

Captain's ship continue on after his loss. Chandra was last aboard, and she took one last look to be certain they were ready to leave before hitting the door switch. Chandra looked around to see that the corridor was empty of all but Taylor.

"All are aboard and gearing up."

"Good, let's join them. There are too many uncertainties in this mission. I want compression suits on before we've left the atmosphere and kept on, as well as masks and tanks kept to hand."

Taylor nodded in agreement as they turned and made their way to the store rooms to gather what they needed. The ship lifted off just seconds later but was so smooth they barely noticed.

Ten minutes later they were ascending from Earth's atmosphere and felt the gravity reduce in the moments before the gravity generators got to full strength and balance.

"I never thought we'd see the day when we went to war in space," said Chandra.

"The day was inevitable. I just would have seen it more likely as a fight between humans. The existence of these creatures still seems unreal."

"I think it'll be a long time before any of what has happened sinks in," she replied.

They went silent for a moment as they each reflected on the last year that had seen more bloodshed than they could ever have imagined.

"Do you think they'll be ready for us? On L2?" asked Taylor.

"No. I would be, but this enemy, they seem arrogant. We have caught them off guard countless times because of their underestimation of the human race, and its ability to adapt and survive. One day they may learn, but I think right now we still have a good chance of getting this station without too much of a fight."

"I bloody hope so. Without it, we'll have a hard time ever getting the Moon back. We're gonna have to use mostly civilian freighters as it is."

She sat back and sighed.

"Maybe we were stupid to not prepare ourselves for this whole eventuality. Look how many times in history great civilisations have been destroyed by such an invasion by an unknown enemy. What did we ever do to prepare for this? We have few military spacecraft. No defence systems, nothing."

"I don't think it'd have made any difference," replied Taylor. "We barely got by in this war with everything we had. Whatever happened, this was always going to be a war fought on our own soil."

She looked and smiled. "Not for much longer."

It felt like a long trip to reach the station when it was in reality just a few hours. Sat in their full gear and with weapons at the ready made them all anxious, but it was necessary the Colonel had said. None of them doubted her after knowing what a danger the enemy could pose. Eventually, Lieutenant Ryan called for the Colonel over the intercom. She was loathed to leave the troops during their journey unless it was necessary. She paced uneasily up to the bridge, knowing the news could only be that the fight was imminent.

Chandra stepped out onto the bridge with Taylor at her side. Before them was a projection of what they were approaching.

"We're coming up fast on the target, Ma'am."

"What are your orders?" she asked him to verify.

"To drop you off a mile out and hold to provide support," he quickly replied.

"Good. Watch out for anyone trying to escape. I don't want any of those bastards getting free and clear of here."

"Yes, Ma'am."

"How long do we have?"

"We'll be at the drop off co-ordinates in fifteen minutes."

"Thank you, Lieutenant."

She lifted her comm. and immediately called out her orders.

"We're dropping in fifteen. All Inter-Allied are to emplane. All pilots to their craft."

She turned back to the Lieutenant. The young officer seemed unfazed by the impending danger they faced. It was a confidence that she admired and could already see that he had followed in Reyes' footsteps.

"Good luck, Lieutenant."

"And to you, Ma'am, I wish you a quick victory and that you all stay safe."

* * *

"We're good to go!" yelled Eddie.

His words resounded around the copter of soldiers who sat in silence awaiting the battle which would ensue.

"Let's get going!"

Taylor and Chandra smiled at the pilot's easy going nature. He always calmed the situation with his relaxed personality at just the right moment. A second later, their engines fired up, and they raced from the docking bay out into the blackness of space. The only thing visible before them was the lights of the station. She pulled her helmet over her head and replaced the helmet on top.

The mask was close fitting and sealed to her compression suit at the neck line. The face was completely visible through the large transparent faceplate. The others quickly followed suit; the thought of asphyxiation in space was a fearful one for the Earthers who had never had to consider such a natural danger.

The two officers could see through Eddie's cockpit and onwards as a light flashed up ahead.

"What the hell is that?" asked Taylor.

They could see the light getting closer, and it was joined by another.

"Incoming!" Eddie shouted.

He reacted quickly, and the copter banked heavily and narrowly avoided the pulse that burnt the surface of their fuselage.

"You said L2 had no defences!" Eddie said.

"It didn't!" shouted Chandra.

"Fuck, this ain't gonna be a walk in the park," replied Taylor.

He turned and looked out of a porthole to see dozens of other craft flying in formation with them. A second later, one of the pulses crashed into a copter and blew the engines off its structure, sending it tumbling out of control. Chandra strained herself to watch the stricken ship.

"Looks like they'll be alright," stated Taylor. "The support ships will pick 'em up."

Chandra slumped back down with a sombre look about her face. Taylor could see that she was beginning to remember what the war had felt like, and she didn't like it one bit. They banked hard several times as they approached and were soon at the station unharmed. Just as they were about to land on the superstructure a porthole was lit up by an explosion, and one of the copters blew up at their flank. Taylor took just a quick glance to see remains of the craft drift past them and narrowly miss Rains' cockpit.

"That one of ours?" Chandra asked.

Taylor nodded solemnly.

"One of Jackson's! Looks like there are survivors."

She looked out of her window to see several soldiers floating in space as they zoomed past. At least a good number seemed to still be moving, and she took solace in knowing they could survive long enough to get picked up, providing they saw victory that day. Chandra shook her head at the losses before they'd even reached their target.

"If they've gone as far as fitting defences, you can be damn sure they're ready to give us a hard time on the ground," Taylor said.

"There is no ground anymore, Major. We left the sensibilities of firm ground sometime ago," she replied.

He smiled in response, but he wasn't at all amused. The idea of space travel never sat well with him. Fighting in the uncertainties of space was something he'd have avoided at all costs, but that was not for him to decide.

"This is it!" yelled Eddie.

The engines rushed into reverse thrust, and the copter rocked as it landed with a solid clunk, latching itself to the outer structure of the station. Chandra leapt to her feet.

"Breach it!"

Doors opened on the floor of the copter and revealed an access tunnel that had extended from their craft. Corporal Hall manoeuvred a shaped charge on an extended bracket down the corridor until it clamped to the structure of the station. He looked up and nodded to the Colonel that they were ready.

"Do it!"

He pressed the trigger, and the small blast punctured through the outer skin with minimal effort. Hall waited for the dust to settle for just a moment to check the breach.

"We're in business!"

"Go, go, go!" shouted Chandra.

The two platoons aboard rushed down the joining corridor and into the station. Chandra and Taylor got through after the first dozen troops and stood in surprise in a corridor to see no sign of movement other than themselves.

"This is Alpha1, we have breached and have met no resistance, over."

She waited just a moment as the rest of the troops took up positions along the ribbed corridor. The large bracing structures allowed a natural defence. She got no response and got no radio traffic at all.

"God damn it, I thought our people had sorted this jamming out?"

Taylor shrugged his shoulders but was not at all surprised. She looked over to him.

"Alright, Taylor you can take them forward from here. Try and link up with the rest Alpha."

The corridor was five metres wide, and clearly a main

access route throughout the structure. Taylor paced forward to lead the two platoons with Chandra close by. They had got just a few metres when they heard rapid gunfire and shouts up ahead. The troops all instinctively dropped down to one knee and took cover.

"Must be Jones."

"They clearly didn't get the smooth entry we did. Move forward and provide assistance. I'll bring up the rear."

Taylor nodded before getting to his feet and beckoning for the troops to move forward with him. He rushed on at a jogging pace and quickly heard the fighting beyond get louder until he could no longer hear his own footsteps. They took a bend, and his heart raced as they came across twenty Mechs spread out through a large circular trading room. Jones' troops had only just managed to breach and get a dozen troops a foothold. They were dug in under heavy fire, and one lay dead on the floor up ahead.

Taylor leapt into the cover of a large desk unit as they came out into the opening of the trading area and lifted his hand to draw them all to a halt. He looked back and beckoned for them to move forward with caution. He lifted his rifle and quickly took aim at the first creature that he had a clear view of from its flank.

"Fire!" he ordered.

Mitch immediately fired five rounds into the chest of the creature he could see the most of, and a final one through its faceplate to be certain. The beast dropped lifelessly to the ground as the others joined in. Dozens of rounds tore into the enemy, but they quickly took better cover as five of their comrades were dropped.

"Get those shields up here!"

The three soldiers carrying the Reitech shields rushed forward. They were all that could be taken with the confines of space.

"Grenades!" Taylor shouted.

"You sure?" asked Hall.

"The station can take it. Do it!"

He continued firing as five grenades were launched over their positions and erupted in the centre of the room.

"Forward!"

The shield bearers rushed forward, and Taylor leapt over the desk he was using for cover. A pulse rushed towards him but was caught just in time by one of the shields. The round crashed into the shield and burst into sparks that sprayed over the Major and burnt a few millimetres into his body armour.

A dozen troops followed him and fired as they advanced with the shield bearers at the forefront and joining in. The brutal volley of fire caught two of the creatures as they tried to rise up from cover and return fire. The fire intensified as Jones and several of his troop advanced from their battered positions.

Taylor's magazine ran dry, and he ducked down behind the next layer of cover and was joined by the others. A few light pulses raged overhead as the pressure was taken off their foes. Taylor slammed in a new magazine and lifted himself, taking a quick aim at a creature. He fired two shots into its head, ducking quickly back down as a pulse flew overhead and skimmed the table where he was taking cover.

He looked back at the next wave of troops who had taken up their old positions; then back to see the first advance he had led were all hunkered down. He gestured to the others to fire over their heads, and it was quickly done. Rifle fire rushed over their heads as they waited their moment to strike. After a few dozen volleys, he lifted his hand to call a halt to their fire.

"Advance!"

He leapt up and jumped onto the table top, affording him a view of several of the Mechs from the vantage point. He stepped confidently forward as he poured fire into their positions. He snapped around as he caught movement, firing on full auto into a creature as it lifted up beside him. It dropped dead before it could even train its weapon on him.

The troops around him poured forward into the enemy positions and finished off the surviving Mechs. Taylor watched and grinned at the defeated foes before them. He turned back to the body lying on the floor in front of the breach. The Major jumped from the table and strolled over to the body of the lifeless soldier who had only gotten a metre from the breach before being struck down.

Jones joined the Major as he knelt down and rolled over the fallen soldier. Smoke still arose from the impact as the body rolled over; it was Blinker. His eyes flicked open, and he stared into the eyes of Mitch.

"Not dead yet, Sir," he spluttered.

Taylor smiled as he hauled the man to his feet. Blinker coughed and sighed in pain, but his wounds were only minor. Monty rushed to his side and slapped him across the back of his helmet.

"Bloody idiot, getting shot like that!"

"I'll try not to next time," he replied.

Taylor turned back, relaxing at the realisation that they were not a man down. He looked to Chandra as she strode down the corridor, scanning the scene of carnage. Then gunfire erupted in far away rooms and echoed down the several corridors which the hall led to.

"Fight isn't over," she stated. "Assemble the troops. Jones, you take half the Company down corridor 17B. We'll take 17A."

Jones quickly nodded to show he had understood and turned to relay his orders.

"1st and 2nd Platoon, on me!" he yelled.

"3rd and 4th, follow me!" Chandra shouted.

They quickly formed up in the market area as they changed their magazines and prepared to move onwards. Chandra and Taylor waited either side of a two metre corridor. She pulled out a Mappad and quickly studied it.

"We're about five hundred metres from the command centre, but it's three floors down. I want command of this station ASAP. There are stairs here and here. You take the first with 3rd Platoon, and I'll continue on to the next with 4th."

"Got it."

She looked back to see that all eyes were on her and awaiting the advance. She nodded and without a word, stepped forward. They hugged either side of the corridor, all keeping their weapons held at the ready as they advanced. The corridor was eerily quiet, but they could still hear gunfire in the distance. There was a bend up ahead, and they crept slowly towards it until Chandra could edge around the corner for a quick look. She leapt back around as automatic fire rang out, and small pulses smashed into the corner where her head had been a second before.

"Christ! Looks like some kind of sentry gun!"

Taylor leapt to her side of the corridor and drew out his Mappad. He pulled out a telescopic camera, twisted a kink into it, and held the edge to the corner. The camera displayed the view beyond onto the device. He got just a few seconds look when a light burst smashed into the camera and wall, tearing the wrecked Mappad from his hands. He quickly ducked back away from the edge.

"Yep, that's something we haven't seen before."

"I guess they weren't on the defensive before," she

replied.

"We could advance with the cover of the shields?"

"No, I don't think they'd withstand the output of that thing."

"Then what do you reckon?"

She took a deep breath, but before she could find an answer, they heard a rush of gunfire emanate from the parallel corridor Jones' had taken. Chandra took a quick look around the corner to see that the sentry gun was engaged in firing at Jones and the others.

"Taylor, I reckon we'll have a few seconds opportunity to lay down fire."

He nodded in return and turned back to the others.

"You three, on the Colonel. When we get round that corner, we give it hell, got it?"

They readied their weapons and grimly agreed, having seen the Colonel almost killed by the fearsome defences.

"Go," she whispered.

Chandra leapt to the far side of the other corridor, allowing them to get an angle on the device. She quickly opened fire, and the others joined in after she'd fired the first shot. A dozen rounds hit the sentry gun's flank that got around the thick frontal shields, but it began to turn for them.

"Keep firing!" she screamed.

She continued to pour fire down the corridor in the hope it would be enough. But by the time the gun had rotated and trained on them, she could already see light building in the barrel. Just as the rounds were about to burst from the barrel, an explosion blasted out from behind the shield of the gun and twisted it into a wreck. Chandra breathed out deeply, knowing how close they had come to death.

"Let's move!" she cried.

The two platoons rushed into the corridor at their backs, and the two officers led from the front at a quick pace. Using their helmet targeting devices, they continued to pour fire down the corridor. They could see Mechs rush to defend against Jones' attack. Taylor had got to the forefront and burst out of the corridor into what was a bar and restaurant district. Light pulses and muzzle flashes lit up the vast space, and Mech bodies were scattered in front of him. He smiled at the sight and lifted his rifle to join in.

Chandra and the others rushed to his side and joined the firing squad. They outnumbered the Mechs in a vast way, but it didn't make them feel any sympathy for the creatures. Over the gunfire, they could just about hear Monty and Blinker yelling insults at the tops of their voices as they gunned down the beasts.

Finally, when the gunfire subsided, they turned to see two of their dead amongst Jones' troops. Chandra shook her head in sadness, but she knew it was only inevitable. She was only thankful they hadn't lost more.

"We're not far from the command centre, let's move!"

They rushed down a corridor at the far side of the sector and reached the stairs as planned. Taylor was descending to the control point and was eager to get there first to deal out some more pain. He reached the semi transparent doors at the base of the stairway and could see that they were sealed shut. Without breaking stride, he fired three shots into the toughened glass and then leapt at it. His body weight ruptured through the fractured plastic, and he tumbled into a roll. Taylor nimbly landed on one knee and was quickly back to his feet.

Three creatures stood before him. One wore ornately inscribed armour that was reminiscent of Karadag's, and his face was visible. The other two creatures displayed the painted red lines, clearly representing their importance as some form of guard to a senior officer or official. For a moment, the two groups looked at each other in amazement.

"Lower your weapons!" he shouted.

He surprised himself to even say it. He'd never met one of the creatures that he wouldn't have shot on sight if he could. They hesitated, but he could see they knew there was little other choice beyond death.

"Lower them!"

The two guards looked to their master, who after a few seconds of thought, nodded for them to comply.

"You would let us live?" asked the enemy Commander.

"I'm here to win this war, not eradicate your race."

Taylor could see the two guards look at each other as if surprised, but he could not see their faces beneath their armour. Gunfire rang out, and plastic shattered as Chandra breached the other entrance and rushed into the room with her rifle at the ready. Taylor held up his hand to stop her. She quickly came to a halt and looked on at the situation in shock.

"What's going on?" she asked.

"I believe these soldiers are surrendering to us."

"Surrender? And what would you have us do with them?"

Taylor lowered his rifle and paced across the room, so he could talk more privately with the Colonel.

"These are soldiers just like us. Wouldn't you want your foe to take mercy if you were cornered? We're better than this, Chandra."

She looked down and cursed. She knew he was right.

"Alright, alright. Find them somewhere secure, and I mean secure. They are to be kept under guard and watched at all times."

"Alright," he replied.

"Looks like we've got most of the station under control. They can't have had more than a hundred or two guarding the whole place."

"Maybe because it was the last thing they ever expected of us?" replied Taylor.

"Alright. Jones, send runners to find Commander Kelly, and notify him we have taken the HQ. 3rd and 4th platoon are to take up positions here. Jones, rally up with Jackson. You're on sweep and clear."

She turned and looked at the three aliens who were still stood waiting to hear of their fortune.

"Taylor, they're your responsibility."

CHAPTER NINE

Taylor had found a temporary holding cell just a few metres from the command centre and had quickly acquired it for his new prisoners. He sat and watched them through a one way screen. Never before had he been able to so closely study one of the creatures while it was still living. He could tell the one creature was of great importance, and he was more than a little curious to understand how much so. The door beside him opened, and Chandra stepped through with Kelly at her side.

The Commander gasped as he saw the three creatures beyond the screen and just a few metres away. He froze for a moment and was clearly thinking of reaching for a weapon before he calmed himself.

"What the hell are they doing here?"

"They surrendered to me, Sir."

"Surrendered? There is no surrender in this war, Major."

Taylor stepped past the Commander and closed the door behind him before stepping back to his previous position.

"If I may, Sir?"

"Go on."

"This creature is clearly of importance among our enemy. It poses no threat to us, and it makes sense to try and learn what we can while we have the opportunity. We are forever lacking information and understanding of these creatures. Would you not like some information on enemy strength, positions?"

Kelly turned and carefully studied the creature that sat against the wall. Its towering frame made the room look out of scale. The beast appeared humbled for having been captured but still proud.

"What makes you think anything it says will be truthful?"

"No idea, but it costs us nothing to talk."

Kelly gritted his teeth, and Mitch could see the Commander hated their enemy more than any of them.

"Alright, but you handle this. I want proper security on these creatures at all times. If this goes sour, it's on you."

"Thank you, Sir."

Kelly strode out of the room, leaving Chandra watching the creatures in amazement. She turned to Taylor.

"Don't take any chances with them. They'd just as soon as rip your head from your body if they had the chance."

"I know," he replied.

"I'll admit I am a little curious. Let me know anything interesting that you discover."

The two of them stepped out of the room where a dozen soldiers were stood either on guard of the room or awaiting the Colonel as her protection. She quickly left with her entourage, leaving Taylor to the interrogation. It was the first communication they'd ever had with the enemy, but it had seemed of little importance once their intentions were clear.

"Hall, get two others and join me. I want you to have your wits about you at all times."

"On it, Sir."

Taylor stepped over to the entrance where Parker and another guarded the entrance.

"Watch your ass in there, Mitch."

"Don't worry, I will."

He opened the security door and stepped inside with the three marines at his back, their weapons raised and ready to fire at a moment's notice. The three creatures sat at the far end of the cell and didn't respond to the presence of the troops. He couldn't tell if they had simply given up and accepted their fate, or if they were biding their time for the right opportunity to strike.

The holding chamber was eight by five metres and allowed them to keep a good distance apart. In the centre of the room was a table with four chairs. Taylor strolled forward and took the nearest seat. The enemy officer looked up and into the eyes of Taylor. He could see some kind of pipe rising around the creature's head from around the suit and into its nostrils. He imagined they couldn't breathe air alone.

"My name is Major Taylor, 2nd Inter-Allied Battalion."

The creature still glared at him but had not moved. It finally opened its mouth and spoke in the same deep and coarse voice that Taylor had heard before.

"The slayer of Karadag."

The creature was relaxed and confident.

"I was there when he was defeated, yes."

"How? How could you, weak and small, kill a hero?"

Taylor's eyes squinted, and his face crunched up in anger.

"Your Karadag was a genocidal maniac. It was an honour to see him to his end."

The beast went silent as it dipped its head and seemed to reflect on his words. Taylor marvelled at how human the creature seemed. They were so different to humans, yet they seemed to have so much in common. Taylor could read the same body language and interaction as if the beast was human.

"Who are you?" asked Taylor.

"Demiran, leader of the 62nd Group, and honoured to be of Karadag's kin."

Taylor's eyes widened. He wondered why the creature had not yet tried to kill him, knowing what he now did.

It made him clench his fists and grow more guarded and ready for anything.

"Why did you surrender to us?"

The creature sat up tall and proud.

"You gave us the chance to live, did you not?"

"We don't kill those who do not fight against us."

"Then that is your mistake."

Taylor smiled. "Need I remind you of who is winning this war?"

Demiran looked away as if shamed. Taylor could tell the leader's guards were confused by the whole conversation. They could clearly understand what was being said, but not why.

"Can there never be peace between our two races?"

"Yes, when we rule your planet."

Taylor shook his head. He'd always hoped that peace could be negotiated, but he had not yet seen any evidence that it was a possibility.

"What are your people's intentions now?"

"Is is not already clear?"

Taylor stood up quickly in frustration at the lack of co-operation.

"How many soldiers do you have on the Moon?"

Demiran glared at him, and it was clear an answer would never come.

Taylor turned in frustration. *I wasn't born for this shit. We need an interrogator,* he thought.

He paced out of the room and returned to the station HQ to find it was now a hive of activity. Kelly and Chandra were busy chatting over a briefing table with four other officers. The Commander noticed as he entered.

"Major Taylor, join us please."

Mitch could make out the insignia of the Moon colony forces on two of the officers, and they glared at him as if he were the enemy, but Kelly welcomed him with open arms.

"Did you get anything from the prisoners?" he asked.

"Nothing useful, Sir. He is a relation of Karadag. I don't think he'll give me anything."

Chandra's eyes widened. "No, you might be able to use that to your advantage."

Kelly thought about it for a moment and nodded in agreement.

"It's true. His anger towards you could let certain information slip, so keep at it. Now, we've secured the station, and Earth has been notified. So far, we have eight dead and thirty-four wounded. It's a solid start. We've got eight hours until the main fleet arrives. Most of the ships will be civilian and unarmed, so it is vital they have a clear run."

"Commander!"

Doyle, Kelly's comms officer spun around in his chair and frantically called out. The Commander turned as the man blurted out the news.

"Sir, we've got incoming!"

Kelly rushed over to the man, and the others stood anxiously awaiting more information.

"Several dozen ships are approaching from the Moon."

"My, God, how long do we have?"

"At the speed they're travelling, maybe two hours."

Kelly turned in horror. He quickly snapped out of it and strode back to the table where the other officers were stood in shock.

"What do you reckon they want? To destroy the station or take it back?" he asked.

"They must have occupied it for a reason," replied Chandra.

"And we have Demiran," Taylor added.

Kelly looked at the Major with a puzzled expression for a second before he clarified.

"The enemy officer we captured."

Kelly shook his head. "To hear their names, it almost makes them feel like a human enemy."

"Sir, we must hold this station, or there is little hope of taking back your homeland. Let alone the fact we cannot let a sizeable enemy force loom over Earth."

He once again snapped out of his daze and turned to the Colonel.

"Of course we must defend it! Captain Morris. We were hit by a defence grid installed by the enemy on our approach. Figure out where it is and get it working.

Chandra, get all combat ships flying, and have them take up defensive positions around the station. Taylor, you've successfully faced off against these bastards more than any of us. I want you to liaise with all other officers on organising the defences. I'll return once I have reported to General Schulz."

The Commander turned and quickly rushed off to Doyle to organise an urgent transmission he would take in a private room. They all knew what it would entail, a desperate bid for support at all haste. Chandra left the table also to go about her business, and Taylor looked up to several confrontational faces. The Earth officers among them admired him, but the Moon Defence personnel despised him to the core.

"Perera, is it? Can you bring up a map of the station?"

The Lieutenant obliged but remained silent. A few seconds later, a digital 3D model of the station was projected above the table up to chest height.

"We still don't know the enemy's intentions. If they mean to destroy this station, then we best hope the Navy boys can do their best. But knowing their tactics, I would expect them to breach with infantry forces, whether they intend to destroy us or merely rescue their officer. Either way, we must prepare for a serious fight."

"Not our first time," replied Perera.

Taylor sighed at the man's insubordinate and snarky comment.

"Let's get something straight. You barely survived and escaped from your colony with the help of our forces. We aren't here to survive by the skin of our teeth. We're here to win. You can either skulk around, and keep bitching like a school boy, or you can join the winners."

Several of the Earth officers could not conceal their amusement that only served to infuriate the Moon officer further.

"What?" Taylor asked. "You want to hit me? You want to kill me? Good, vent that at the enemy. I don't give a shit what you feel towards me. I am here to serve a purpose. Fall in line, or get out of my sight!"

The Lieutenant knew he had been unprofessional and unhelpful and so felt uneasy, but Taylor could still see the hatred in his eyes.

"Right, let's get on with what's at hand."

He quickly studied the map of the station and could see that it was a vast area to have to cover.

"We're gonna be spread a little thin. If they were going to set charges to blow this place, you can bet your ass it'll be either at the energy and grav generators here, or the central engineering quarters here. Those will be our focus points, as well as the command centre and guarding of the prisoners."

"Is it wise to leave so much of the station unguarded?"

Taylor looked to the Asian man but couldn't identify his rank from an insignia that he did not recognise.

"Sorry, but I do not believe we have met."

"Colonel Chen."

"You fought with the MDF?"

"A hard struggle."

Taylor could see the Colonel had no qualms about being under the orders of a less ranked officer. Mitch's reputation still gained him immense respect from most in the military fraternity.

"The incoming forces must have departed the Moon within minutes of our attack, meaning they probably have some idea of our strength. With that in mind, I can guarantee they'll be hitting us hard. If we split our numbers, this station could be overrun, and we'd have nowhere to run."

Mitch studied the map once again before pointing out a number of points.

"I want these corridors sealed off, anyway you can. That'll close off all ancillary districts of the station, leaving us with only a third of the floor space to cover."

"Nothing we do will keep them contained for long," replied Perera.

"No, but time is not on their side. General Schulz is on his way. We only have to hold until he gets here."

"We've got four access points to cover, Colonel Chen. I'd like you here, at hall 14B. The MDF will take the crossroads at the end of hall 86E. Captain Nichols and the Royal Greens will take the engineering levels. 112th

Mechanised, under Major Achen, will cover the corridors leading to the command centre here, and the prisoners themselves.

"Where will you be?" asked Chen.

"We have to be ready for anything. 2nd Inter-Allied will remain fluid for rapid deployment to any breaches, and to provide assistance to any and all locations needing it."

"Trying to be the hero again, everywhere at once?" asked Perera.

Taylor righted himself and took a few quick steps up to the Lieutenant. Perera stood tall in defiance, taunting the Major. Taylor without warning struck the man with a hard punch to the jaw, knocking him to the ground. Mitch had been careful not to use all the power his suit afforded him, which would have been enough to break the man's neck.

"This is not a pissing contest. It's not a game, and I don't have time for it. You don't like me because of what has already happened and I cannot change. Well here's some news for you. You didn't have it worse than everyone else. Man the fuck up, and start acting like god damn soldier!"

Mitch loomed over the Lieutenant, whose nose was bleeding and jaw clearly sore. The man was still stunned and humbled before him.

"There is no room for fighting each other. It will hinder our forces and is an uncertainty none of us can afford. The next insubordinate comment will earn you a place in the brig, where you will sit out this fight and hope there is still someone standing to deal with you after. Now, do I have your allegiance?"

Taylor was sick of trying to pander to some of the MDF troops. He knew he had no other option but to no longer give them a choice. The man begrudgingly nodded in agreement. Mitch offered out his hand to both help the man up and in a gesture of good will. Perera accepted, knowing he had little other choice. He could see in Taylor's eyes that the Major would just as soon shoot him in the head if he continued on his current path. Mitch wrenched the man to his feet and quickly turned back to the others who were still shocked at the sudden violent outburst.

"You know where you are to be. We have to assume that our communications will be jammed. Tap into the station's cabled comms so that we can maintain contact at all times. I also want all platoons to assign a runner to pass on messages, should we lose all contact due to power outage or damage to the station's systems."

He looked at the map one last time.

"You haven't got long. Get those access points sealed up and build what defences you can, that'll be all."

The officers scattered to go about their business. Kelly strode back into the room with a paler face than usual, looking in surprise at Perera's bloody face as the Lieutenant passed him. He didn't interfere or ask after the man. He knew he must leave Taylor to resolve any issues between them. Mitch was the only one left at the table awaiting the

Commander.

"Schulz is going to make all haste, but the best we can hope for is six hours until they arrive. For now we're on our own."

Taylor nodded, but he had already accepted their predicament. He outlined the plans to Kelly in just a few minutes, and they both stood silently staring at the projected map and lost in thought.

"It's a simple plan, as good as can be made," Kelly finally stated.

"Thank you, Sir. I'd like you to stay in overall command here. You'll be able to direct everything from this position through the hard lines and runners."

"Alright, thank you, Major. Please go on and continue with the preparations."

Mitch picked up his rifle and quickly jogged out of the command centre to find several of his troops waiting for him. Ninety minutes later, they were as prepared as they could hope to be. Taylor and Chandra were side by side in a corridor junction. The Battalion had been spread out across three floors and multiple points in order to act as intended.

"Sure it was wise to split our own and spread them so thin?" asked Chandra.

"We need rapid response teams, and we have the most capable troops for the job."

She nodded in agreement, but she didn't dislike the idea

any less.

The loudhailers fitted throughout every room and corridor crackled as Kelly came on to give his last few words to them all before the battle would begin.

"This is Commander Kelly. Within the next ten minutes, we will face whatever the enemy can throw at us. All we have to do is hold. We have nowhere to run, and nowhere to hide. This station is absolutely essential to winning this war and driving the invaders from our solar system. It must be defended at all costs."

He took a deep breath as he realised he may well be asking them all to fight to their last dying breath.

"A lot is of expected of us all here today. The human race is depending on us to get the job done. Most of you here have lived your whole lives on Earth. I very much appreciate the efforts and sacrifices you are making. But let us not forget, this is not about taking the Moon Colony back. It is about driving this enemy away for good. It is about ensuring they no longer threaten any of our homes ever again!"

The intercom went silent for a moment.

"I have just received word that the enemy craft are entering firing range in three minutes. Be ready for anything. Stand your ground, and remember what we are all fighting for. Any breaches or enemy engagements are to be immediately reported. Let's keep a tight lid on this, good luck to you all!"

The tannoy system fell silent, and the corridors went utterly silent as the soldiers reflected on his words. Finally, Chandra looked to Taylor and broke the silence.

"All that we have survived, and now we find ourselves locked up in a tin can with nothing around us but space. I don't like fighting when there is no escape by land or sea."

"Agreed, but I remember you being eager to get into space."

She chuckled.

"Eager to kill those bastards, certainly. Let's not let it end up here, okay? If I'm gonna die in this war, I want it to be of firm ground."

"Amen to that. Why on Earth anyone ever wanted to live on the God damn Moon is a mystery to me."

The two of them had each attached themselves to a platoon of Jones' Company. The Captain waited on a floor down with the other two platoons in readiness for the rapid deployment which they expected to need. The Commander's voice came over the tannoy once again.

"Enemy targets have entered firing range. We have incoming fire!"

In the confines of the station, they could neither hear nor see any of what was going on. They wondered whether they'd want to see it, or if it was worse to have to wait to see the fate of themselves and their friends. Mitch finally broke and couldn't withstand it any longer. Eddie was out there fighting alongside so many other pilots and Navy personnel he called friends.

"Fuck this, I want to see what's happening!"

He leapt to his feet, and Chandra did not have the heart to stop him. Mitch made it down two corridors with several troops in tow before finally reaching an area with portholes giving a view to the outside world; light pulses from both the enemy and friendly weapons. Before he could identify any of the lightning fast battle in front of him, he was drawn to an object approaching their position at rapid velocity.

His eyes widened as he realised it was an enemy craft heading right for them on a deliberate path. He turned quickly with just enough time to warn those around him.

"Incoming!"

He leapt a few steps away from the window to take cover, but the explosion he had expected never came. He stood up in surprise as a loud clang rang out as something clamped onto the hull of the station. A small blast vibrated the corridor around them. A large plate of corridor burst inwards just ten metres away from the Major.

"Breach!" he yelled.

He turned back to Lam stood beside him.

"Get the Colonel here, now!"

He turned back and took up position in the ribbing of the corridor wall. He raised his rifle just as he saw the faint but instantly recognisable silhouette of a Mech infantryman appearing through the dust cloud created from the breach. He waited just a second for it to step into the open, and then he took a deep breath.

Here we fucking go again, he thought.

Footsteps pounded down the corridor, and it only intensified the rapid pounding of Taylor's heart he always felt when a fight was about to begin. The creature up ahead turned quickly in his direction as it heard the troops approaching. Without hesitating, Mitch squeezed the trigger and loosed off a volley of shots, riddling the creature with bullets.

Before the beast had hit the deck, another two had advanced past it, and Taylor heard the rapid fire of weapons beside him. He'd prayed their fleet outside was still in the fight, but he no longer had the time to think of them. A light pulse rushed down the corridor between the troops huddling in against the ribbing of the corridors that provided them with some useful cover. Two more of the creatures were killed before Taylor's eyes as he continued to pour fire down the corridor.

He could see they had a solid defence, and his people were more than capable of holding. It was his opportunity to get back to Chandra and check on any news. Just after a pulse flew past his position, he rushed out and quickly dived around the corner where Chandra was waiting.

"I've already had word sent to Jones to box them in the other end!" she shouted.

"So they are jamming us?"

She nodded in response.

"Are the hard lines still working?"

"For now. Do you think you can hold them in that corridor?" she asked.

"No problem, but it's not this breach I'm worried about. It's the next one and the one after."

Chandra dipped her head and sighed at the desperation of their situation, and Taylor could already see she knew more than she had said.

"What is it?"

"We already have two other breaches."

"Christ, I bloody hope Schulz gets a God damn shift on! How are the other breaches holding?"

"So far they're holding. But Mitch, I don't know how many more of these we can take. Info is still sketchy on the enemy strength, but clearly what we have in the air isn't enough to hold them off."

Taylor thought back to Rains for a minute. He knew the pilots and Navy personnel were their first line of defence, and so would be getting it the worst. Part of him hoped they had beaten a hasty retreat and saved themselves from the bitter onslaught of the aliens, but more than anything he prayed they had stayed. Corporal Hall rushed up to stand between the two officers and blurted out his news before they could ask his purpose.

"Colonel, we have another two breaches, one on this deck and one on 2A."

"Alright, Kelly will have to handle one. We'll take this level."

She turned to Taylor. "Can you handle this, here?"

He nodded quickly in response.

"Alright, we'll head to the other breach. Pray for us all, Major. Pray we make it through this. Pray the enemy are in few numbers, and pray Schulz is as quick to respond as we might hope."

"Too much to chance, Colonel. I'll rely on me and my own, first and foremost. Let's show these bastards why you don't mess with the human race!"

He turned and rushed back to his positions to peel off half the platoon to continue on to the new destination. He knew he was spreading their troops thin, but there was little else to do.

"Hall, we've got to move, now!"

The Corporal turned to look at the battle ensuing ahead where Jones had clearly flanked the enemy and engaged them with a brutal salvo of fire.

"The Captain can handle this, come on!"

Taylor led just twelve men to the next breach. Hall led the section he now commanded; a corporal was all they could muster anymore.

"Sir, we can't keep covering so much ground!" yelled Hall as they rushed down a narrow corridor.

"We have to. We have to hold!"

"Spread this thin, one break in our line, and we'll be

fucked!"

"That's a chance we'll have to take, Corporal. Now haul ass and give 'em hell!"

* * *

"Morris! Get down that corridor and cut them off!" Kelly shouted.

The Commander was stood at the entrance to the command centre with rifle in hand. A fallen Mech lay just twenty metres down the corridor. He shook his head in disbelief at how close the enemy had got. Martinez rushed to his side. The officer had blood splattered across his face, but it was clearly not his own.

"Sir, you must get back in to the CP. We can handle it here!"

Kelly looked around and initially thought to lash out at the man for tell him what to do. But he thought for just long enough to appreciate it had to be done.

"Alright, but you get back to the fight. Don't let any of those bastards near the holding cell. Those prisoners may be the only reason we're still alive!"

He quickly turned and rushed back into the command post to see Lewis receiving frantic communications from around the station. Kelly could do nothing but stand beside him and await the news. Eventually, the comms officer looked up and reported with a stunned and grim tone.

"Sir, we've got five breaches. Two are within the containment areas, but I have lost the video feeds."

Then you can bet your arse they'll be banging on the doors soon enough. Where are they likely to try and break through?"

Lewis leapt to his feet and strode over to the projected map of the station.

"The enemy craft that breached within the confinement areas are here, and here. Captain Nichols will have to face one, the other force is coming for us."

"Alright, let Major Achen know. How is Perera doing?"

"Only light contact so far."

"And the Navy boys?"

"From what I can see, they're still slugging it out. They have been able to stop a number of the assault ships, but clearly they're still getting through."

The room shook violently as a blast rang out just ten metres from where they were stood. The two of them ducked instinctively as items on the desk beside them were launched onto the deck.

"What the fuck was that?" yelled Kelly.

He heard a myriad of shots and screams ring out from the corridor outside, and it was followed by automatic weapon fire.

"They must have breached the adjacent corridor, Sir," replied Lewis.

"God damn it! Get Taylor and tell him we need assistance, now!"

CHAPTER TEN

A comms unit flashed on the wall opposite where Taylor was huddled.

"Hall! Get that call!"

The Corporal looked at the Major for a second in astonishment. Dust and debris still floated around the corridors, and they were still taking fire. A pulse had hit the wall next to the unit just twenty seconds earlier.

"Get the God damn call, Corporal!"

Hall didn't hesitate a second time. He leapt across the open corridor, and hit the open channel key.

"This is the CP, we need immediate assistance. I repeat, immediate assistance! We have a breach at 2A, and Achen is tied up!"

Taylor could hear the desperate call, even from the other side of the corridor and over the noise of the battle.

"We're on our way! Hold on!"

He turned to Chandra, but she responded before he could ask the question.

"We've got it here, go!" she shouted.

"3rd platoon, on me!" he cried.

Taylor rushed to the stairwell, knowing none of them could risk using the elevators. He leapt four steps at a time and rushed so quickly through the automatic doors that he buckled them as his exosuit caught the frame either side. As he burst into the corridor, he caught sight of a Mech and quickly fired as he passed to the other side of the corridor, unable to stop himself with the momentum. Mitch saw his round land wide of its target, but it was enough of a distraction to get him safely behind cover.

As he smashed into the far wall, he lifted up his hand to signal for the others to stop as three energy bursts rushed down the corridor between them.

"Jesus Christ!" Hall screamed, and he stopped just in time to save having his head blown off. He backed up against the side of the doorway Taylor had only moments before smashed in passing. He quickly reached for a grenade, but Taylor noticed as he was about to twist the firing cap.

"No grenades!"

Hall looked down at the grenade, looking sheepish for a moment for not remembering. He slipped the grenade back onto his webbing as pulses continued to fly down the gap between the two men. They could tell the enemy were advancing towards them because the pulsating of their weapons was getting louder with each shot.

"What do we do, Sir?" asked Hall.

"Get the rest of the platoon out here, and start fucking shooting! We can't let them continue!"

The Corporal spun around and barked with the same ferocity as his Major had.

"Move your fucking asses and get up there! The Major is under fire!"

Taylor leaned out and took a few quick shots but was under too much pressure from enemy pulses to make any targeted fire. Hall leapt from the doors and rushed a few metres forward with his head hunkered down until he could leap into cover behind the next rib of the corridor. Just as he got to the cover, a pulse smashed the rim of the rib and blew a football-sized chunk from the side. Hall gasped as the debris burst past, realising how close he had come to death.

Another six soldiers got into the corridor and started laying down fire. It finally freed Taylor up to take some aimed shots. His next two rounds went directly through the faceplate of one of the Mechs and killed it instantly.

"How many do you count?" Taylor shouted to Hall.

"I guess about another six!"

"We need this dealt with! If we don't get to the CP soon, this could all be over!"

He turned to the other troops still huddled in the

doorway.

"I want you to get out here and lay down concentrated fire on my go!"

The two at the front nodded in agreement. There was no fear in their eyes, and he was glad to see that they trusted him completely.

"Now!"

Three of the soldiers leapt out from the corridor, and Taylor immediately jumped up from his cover and began firing rapidly. They were quickly joined by others as the corridor was flooded with fire. The enemy before them disappeared into a cloud of sparks and smoke. A few last flashes burst from their weapons, and Taylor felt the burn as they rushed past nearby, but he kept on firing. At last, he could tell the opposition had stopped.

"Hold your fire!"

He rushed forward as the dust settled to find that the Mechs were all but finished. One struggled about on the ground, trying to get to its feet but was clearly mortally wounded. Taylor lifted his rifle and put a single shot into its faceplate. The creature dropped to the deck with a heavy crash, and once more the corridor was silent. Taylor turned to see one of their own was on the ground with another giving assistance. He rushed back to the position to see that the man was still conscious.

The man had been struck by a pulse that had clipped his hip just beneath his torso armour. He grimaced in pain but remained silent. It was clear he was in a lot of pain.

"You'll be okay, but we cannot stop for anything."

"Go, I'll be fine," he replied.

The field medic at his side nodded in agreement and lifted up the man's rifle from the floor, thrusting it into his hands.

"You make sure you nail any alien bastard that comes this way, you hear?" insisted Taylor.

"You got it, Sir," he replied, hoisting the rifle up into both hands.

Taylor looked to the others around him and could see they were appalled at having to leave one of their own behind. He hated himself doing it, but he diverted that hatred to their enemy for forcing his hand.

"Let's move!"

They quickly got up to pace and were well on their way to the CP when they heard a hail of gunfire beneath them on the next level down. Taylor stopped for a moment, knowing it would be their friends and comrades in action. He knew they could not assist, but for a second he considered it. The looks on the faces of the troops around him showed they all shared the same concern.

"They can handle themselves, just as we can," he mused quietly to those closest. He continued onwards and quickly came upon a fight close to the CP. In the corridor were four bodies of Perera's troops, and clearly the rest had beaten a hasty retreat against overwhelming numbers.

Only two Mechs lay dead around them.

"Fuck, this must have been bad."

"God damn idiot, I told him to stand his ground," Taylor caught a glimpse of movement up ahead and looked up to see a Mech stroll past at the end of the corridor, firing as it did.

"Christ this is a total cluster fuck. Let's clean this up!"

He strode forward with his rifle held low and forwards, ready to blast the nearest foe he could find. They got within just fifty metres of the CP when they came up on the flank of an enemy force that was besieging the dug in MDF soldiers. Taylor lifted his hand to call them to a halt.

"They've not noticed us yet, so fortune is on our side if we move quickly. We do not stop until we are on top of them, you hear?"

Hall nodded and turned to see the nearest of them had too. It was enough to keep the momentum going. Taylor nodded to confirm to go ahead and was first in line heading to towards the enemy at a quick jogging pace. A few moments later, he opened fire and kept it up without slowing.

The five men at the head of the platoon fired relentlessly as they continued forward at a quick pace. Three of the creatures were killed by the time Mitch had emptied his magazine. Without slowing his pace, he hit the release catch, and slammed in a fresh magazine. He was back on the trigger within a second of the first round being chambered.

They had caught the unit of Mechs utterly by surprise, and it was clear the friendly troops they had been assaulting had seized the opportunity to brutalise their attackers. The Mech position was hit by a barrage of fire. Still Taylor did not slow his pace and ran right up to the last creature, firing repeatedly at it. Finally, he dropped his rifle so that it slung to his side and drew out his Assegai. He leapt up onto the beast and thrust the weapon down through its armour into its head. The beast collapsed down with him still holding on.

The fire had stopped and all had frozen in amazement at the brutality and unwavering determination of Taylor. He stood up and drew his weapon from the beast. Upon seeing the thick dark blood dripping from the blade, he spat on the body of the creature in disgust.

He looked up just in time to see Perera turn and rush back towards the CP. Some of his men followed, but the others were still in shock and staring at the Major.

"Where the fuck's he going?"

They looked at him in silence.

"Where?"

"He's gone for those alien bastards we caught."

"Why? What's he gonna do?"

The soldier shrugged his shoulders, but it was clear Perera was going to do what they wanted to.

"For fuck sake, with me, now!"

Taylor barged through the MDF soldiers and continued on in an angry stride that no one dared confront. He passed through a line of Kelly's guards and rushed on through to the holding chamber. He burst through the door to find eight MDF soldiers inside. Perera had a handgun pointed at Demiran's head and was yelling at him.

"Tell your fucking soldiers to fall back! Tell them now!"

The alien sat confidently on the bench where Taylor had last seen him. He had a defiant look upon his face, in spite of the weapon pointed between his eyes.

"Lieutenant!" Taylor shouted.

The man flinched and turned his head quickly at the voice of the man he had come to fear, but he kept the weapon raised.

"Put the gun down!"

The Lieutenant mumbled as he tried to respond, but Taylor just shouted again which made shudder.

"Stand down, Lieutenant! Demiran's survival could be why we're still standing!"

Perera looked conflicted, and in that moment, one of Demiran's guards leapt forward and struck the Lieutenant, causing the gun to fly across the room. He took another step to continue the onslaught, but Taylor leapt in amongst them. He drove a heavy kick into the creature's flank. It crumpled just enough for him to throw it off balance with a heavier barge.

The two other creatures were already on their feet,

but with so many rifles trained on them, they didn't dare move. Perera got to his feet and spat out blood. His nose was broken but not so much as his pride. He stumbled over and snatched up his pistol from the floor. He quickly trained it on the fallen creature as Demiran and the other guard watched.

Taylor turned, saw what was happening, and roared out. "Perera!"

The man turned as Taylor's fist connected with his face. With his other hand, Mitch took hold of the weapon and drove a knee into the Lieutenant's stomach before shoving him down onto his back.

"What the hell do you think you're doing?"

The MDF soldiers quickly raised their rifles against Taylor, and the Major's own men were quick to respond in the same fashion. Perera coughed and spluttered before shouting out in rage.

"You'd take their side over ours! Whose side are you on? You left us to die once, and now you defend these things?"

Taylor looked down in disgust. For a moment, he couldn't even find any words to respond to the man. He couldn't tell which of them hated the other more. The whole scenario struck him as bizarre, when the real enemy stood beside them both and were besieging them as they fought each other.

"I will not have any soldier butchered like some wild

animal," Taylor said calmly.

Perera struggled to his feet and glared at Mitch.

"Have you lost your mind? Look at them! Look! What do you think they are?"

Taylor dipped his head and sighed in disbelief. He didn't even think to reach for his rifle which still dangled at his side. He could not bring himself to aim a weapon at his own.

"You can kill as many of the enemy as you like when you face them in battle. If you want blood, then get out and join the fight. There are enough of the bastards out there. But I will not have you executing anyone. I will not have you destroying assets, and I will certainly not have you questioning my authority!"

"You know this war can't be over until every one of them is dead?" he spat back.

"Look back into our history, Lieutenant. Genocide is not the answer. It's not even possible on such a large scale, and God knows plenty have tried. We can win this war, but there may well come a day when we must talk to these creatures or see the annihilation of both our races."

"You've lost your mind, Major. You are not fit to serve, and I am hereby relieving you of your position in this taskforce until you can face an appropriate tribunal."

Taylor laughed in response.

"I'll never spend another day behind bars because of assholes like you."

Mitch stood tall and looked at the man with disgust. He couldn't believe that in such a dire time of need, he was being so selfish and foolish. But before any of them could speak another word, an explosion erupted at their feet, and the floor around them collapsed. They smashed down to the next level and were stunned by the impact. Taylor's vision and hearing were blurred, but from his back, he could just make out the two enemy bodyguards holding Demiran back from charging at him like a raging bull.

Mitch tried to lift himself up, but he was dizzy and disorientated. His hearing was still shot even with the defence his helmet had given. He tripped, falling back to the ground, and looked up again to see that the three enemies were gone. He faded out into unconsciousness but awoke violently a minute later as Parker slapped him in the face.

"Jesus, Mitch, what the hell happened?"

He shook his head as he tried to regain composure, and she slapped him again a little harder.

"Demiran, where is he?"

"Gone! Jesus, Mitch, we really are in the shit."

"Christ," he replied.

She held out her arm and hoisted him to his feet. He looked around to see Hall was just about on his feet, but one of the MDF soldiers lay dead where part of the floor had crushed his mask and fractured his skull.

"Perera?"

"Was pursuing the prisoners, last I saw."

"What are you doing here?" he asked.

"We were en route to assist at 82A when we heard the blast."

"I have to get back to the CP. This place is going to shit. We need to work out what the hell is going on and rein it all in."

"Alright, I'll go with you."

"No, you were en route to somewhere that needed your help. We're fine, get back to the fight."

It was the last thing he wanted to say to her, but he knew he was right to have faith and put her where she could help most. She leaned in and kissed him before turning and quickly leading her platoon off down a nearby corridor. He watched her leave and prayed it would not be the last time he would see her alive.

* * *

"Fall back! Fall back!" Jones ordered.

Silva was by his side and firing frantically.

"Sir, we haven't got much room left to run," replied Silva.

"I know. Maybe if we can rendezvous with Chen, we might stand a chance, but we can't hold here!"

He looked down the corridor to see five of their unit running back towards him for cover. Light pulses were rushing between them. One of the soldiers was hit in the back. The first round hit his back plate and sent him tumbling to his knees; the second took his head clean off. Jones could see an endless swarm of Mechs advancing through the broad corridor, and it was a fearsome sight.

Silva grabbed the Captain and hauled him from his position as a pulse landed. They felt the hot sparks burn into the armour at their backs, but they didn't stop to check the damage. The two platoons were in full flight. Jones could not help but feel the misery of having to run from an enemy once again; an enemy that only recently they thought they had beaten.

Jones stopped around a corner and let the rest of the troops pass. He and Silva brought up the rear, firing a last few bursts before taking to almost a sprinted speed to reach friendly lines. Up ahead, they could see some of Chen's troops, and they were engaged in a battle in an adjacent corridor.

"We're running out of God damn space to run!" called Silva.

They continued on the Chinese soldiers' positions where Jones finally drew them to a halt.

"Take up positions! Give 'em hell!"

* * *

Taylor rushed into the CP to find it was packed with more

than fifty wounded and had become the only safe med centre on the station. Kelly was busy helping a medic seal a wound and seemed all but to have given up on managing the defence.

"Commander Kelly!"

He didn't respond, and Taylor had no time to waste. He grabbed the Commander by his shoulder and violently tore him from his patient.

"Sir, Demiran has escaped!"

"What? How?"

"Your boy, Perera, God damn amateur. If we don't locate Demiran and stop him from leaving this station, we may as well just lay down and die."

"What are you waiting for? Find him!"

"Sir, we need intel. The station's a complete mess. Nobody knows where enemy and friendly lines are. We need to know where Demiran is, and how we can reach him in the shortest time possible."

Kelly snapped back into action and rushed across to where Lewis stood watching the remaining video feeds in horror. Half of the corridors and rooms were filled with the dead and dying of both races.

"The prisoners have escaped. Find them, now!"

Lewis leapt into action. He flipped through screens at a rapid rate, and within ten seconds he had got a sighting.

"There!"

"Have they found any of their kind yet?"

"Doesn't look like it, Sir. They're somewhere on Level 3, around corridor 12C."

Taylor turned back to find Parker standing beside him.

"I want both platoons ready to move with me. We're going hunting."

He turned back to Lewis.

"We've got no wireless comms, but we'll need information as it changes when we near the escaped prisoners. We'll work from intercom to intercom, track our movements in relation to theirs at all times, and so update us at every opportunity."

"Sir, it's insane. There are Mechs everywhere," he replied.

"If I wanted to do this, yes, it would be insane. But we have no choice."

Taylor lifted his rifle and rushed out of the room. He passed Parker and the others awaiting him without a word, but he knew they'd follow wherever he asked. He had a location to aim for and drove towards it with all determination. Down two of the corridors in the crossroads before the CP he could see the battle still raging. Parker rushed up to his side.

"You really think you can catch them?" she asked quietly.

"We don't have a choice. It's all that matters, right now."

"Then if I was them, I'd be heading for one of the docking bays and getting off this station in the shortest time possible. I'm sure they'd have no problem blowing it to hell once their Demiran is gone. They seem to have no care for their own soldiers."

Taylor stopped near a comms unit and quickly hit the open channel switch.

"Lewis, can you find out where the nearest docking bays are, and if they have enemy craft aboard?"

"Yes, Sir, just give me a moment."

"We're continuing on as planned, so have that info ready for us when we reach our destination."

They continued on down the corridor, but Taylor came to an abrupt halt as two Mechs rushed into the far end of the corridor.

"Shit!"

He leapt aside and called out to the others, giving them just enough time to duck for cover. He peered around the edge of his cover to see that more of the enemy troops were flooding into the corridor.

"Mitch, you need to go on. We'll hold them here!" called Parker.

It was the last thing he wanted to do, and it made him feel sick to have to do it, but he knew she was right. He looked back to Hall who was returning fire down the hallway.

"Corporal, there was a turn twenty metres back. You and your platoon are on mine now!"

Taylor leapt out from the cover and made a break for

it. He heard Eli and her troops open up with covering fire, and it was just enough to pave the way for his retreat. He took the bend quickly and without hesitating to check what was down there. Mitch stopped Hall and the others as soon as they were safe. He took a deep breath and looked down the corridor to see a comms access point.

"Come on, we need a new route through."

He rushed down to the unit that lay at an entrance to a dining hall that was still impeccably laid out as if it had completely passed the war by.

"Lewis, we need a new route through. We're in a large mess hall half way towards our original co-ordinates."

"I've got you, Major, and I've got that intel you asked for."

"Alright, go ahead."

"We've got enemy craft in two docking bays. One is on the other side of the station, and the other is not too far from your current position."

"How do we get there?"

"Get through that hall, and when you come out the other side, take your first left. You'll come into a main access route, larger than the other corridors. From there, you'll have signs to Docking Bay Bravo."

"Good work."

"Good luck, Sir."

Taylor turned back to the others. He had just twenty-five men at his command in a station overrun with enemy forces, and they were against the clock.

"Listen up, we've got no time to spare. We are making a dash for the docking bay. We do not stop. We do not hesitate. Anyone who falls gets left behind. I don't care if that's me or Hall, you keep moving. Someone has to get to that docking bay and stop Demiran. Whatever happens, he must not get off this station, you hear me?"

They nodded solemnly. Taylor quickly turned and jumped to a running pace across the hall. He knew they could come under fire at any moment. All elements of his training would have him check every corner and corridor, but now he had to just keep running and hope for the best. They reached the far door to the hallway, and Taylor barged through, smashing the doors from their frame. He didn't even break stride as the doors flew into the next hallway and crashed to the ground.

"Come on!" he bellowed.

He didn't look back. He had to rely on them to follow him to hell and back. He took the bend as instructed and was quickly out into the main access hall. He could see the sign up ahead for the docking bay and sprinted past it.

"Almost there!"

He took a bend at a large sign, and the doors slid open as the motion sensors detected his position and opened quickly before he could barge through. He stood in the entrance and looked down at the vast docking area for movement. His heart raced as he saw a glimmer of movement near a small enemy ship.

"That's it!"

Before the others could respond, a hail of enemy pulses rushed down the hallway before them. Taylor and Corporal Hall leapt into the cover of the doorway as two of their platoon were struck down, and the others dug in to return fire. Taylor looked back in horror at the realisation that the rest of the troops were stuck where they were. He turned to Hall.

"This is on us, Corporal."

Taylor jumped out and rushed towards the enemy craft. He noticed some activity and turned to see Perera and several of the MDF soldiers closing in on the enemy vessel from another entrance off to his left side.

"Take out the engines!" Taylor shouted.

He saw one of Demiran's guards rush up the access ramp as it quickly clamped up into the craft. The docking doors were already open, and they could see the pulsating of the engines increase as the craft began to lift from the deck. Taylor took quick aim and kept firing until his magazine was empty. They poured fire into the engines until smoke belched from the craft, but it still had forward momentum. He turned to Hall who was changing his magazine.

"Get those doors shut!"

The Corporal sprang into action and rushed for the access panel. Taylor slammed in another magazine and continued to fire rapidly. The small alien fighter was ripped apart by their fire, but they seemed unable to stop it in its tracks.

"If they get into space, we're fucked!" Taylor barked.

Hall ripped open the cover to the panel of controls. He smashed down the large red emergency lockdown button. He turned to see the doors in front of the fighter quickly slam shut, and the locking mechanisms activate. The stricken enemy craft smashed into the doors but crumpled against them without making a dent. The engines powered down as the vehicle rocked back and came to a standstill. The Corporal lifted his rifle back up and loaded in a fresh magazine, following the Major down to the crash site.

Perera and his two comrades closed on the vessel also with their weapons at the ready. Finally, the two groups came together beside it. For the moment, their personal feud was set aside in the presence of a greater threat. The five soldiers stopped with their weapons at the ready and hesitated for a moment, no one wanted the approach the door.

"Oh, fuck this," said Hall.

He paced forward and reached around the corners of the door that jutted out from where their gunfire had torn apart the rear of the ship. Just as he was about to apply some pressure, it was blasted open and crushed him down to the floor. The three creatures rushed from the doorway and fired as they did so. The two soldiers with Perera were struck and killed in a hail of gunfire. Taylor was thrown off his feet by one of the bodyguards that launched him off his feet with a vicious barge. He landed hard and lost consciousness.

A few moments later, Taylor came to his senses and looked up to see the barrel of Perera's gun pointed at him. Flat out on the deck, and still stunned, he was unable to defend himself.

"I knew this day would come, when I could end you. You left our people to die, and now you'll pay the price."

Taylor ignored his comments and replied with a question.

"Where's Demiran?"

"He's gone. It's just you and me now."

Taylor sighed in disbelief. He didn't care for himself, and he only thought of the fate of them all if Demiran had indeed gone.

"Goodbye, Major."

Taylor stared his would be killer in the eyes as the man squeezed the trigger, but as he did so, he was lifted from the ground, and his neck snapped. His body was tossed aside like a ragdoll, and Taylor looked up in fear as one of Demiran's bodyguards stood towering over him. He knew he was at the mercy of the creature, but to his shock it held out its hand as if to help him to his feet.

Confused as to the creature's intentions, Taylor had little choice but to go along with it. He offered up his, and the creature hauled him to his feet with no effort at all. As Taylor landed on his feet, he drew his Assegai and pressed the tip against the rim of the creature's faceplate. Something stayed his hand though, and he held it to threaten but did not strike. The creature had saved his life, and curiosity made him wonder why he had been allowed to live.

The alien before him did not respond to his weapon. Its faceplate quickly retracted and uncovered its face to the Major. Their faces were just twenty centimetres apart, and neither made a move. He took a pace back and slid the Assegai back into its sheath. He was confused by the situation and shocked to still be alive. The other bodyguard walked casually into view, stood beside the other, and likewise revealed its face.

"What are your intentions?" asked Taylor.

The first creature that had helped him finally spoke.

"You saved our lives from your own people, despite all the death and destruction we have brought to your people, why?"

"Because we are all soldiers in this war, and we didn't start the war. And I'd like to think if I were captured, I would be treated in the way in which I would do to others."

The two aliens looked at him, as if utterly confused by what he had said.

"Lord Demiran has escaped. He left us to die here, and yet you let us live. We would serve a master who values our lives like he does his own."

"What are you saying?" asked Taylor.

"That you have our allegiance. You fight beside your soldiers like brothers."

"And you would fight against your own race because of this?"

The creatures nodded in agreement. Mitch studied them intently. He was desperately trying to decide what the best course of action was. It was already clear to him that they were the only reason he was still alive. A cough echoed around the room, and Taylor turned to see that Hall had awoken but was still trapped beneath the ramp of the craft. Taylor looked back to the two creatures, and in that moment decided he needed their help, and that ruled out any other reservations he might have.

"Help me!"'"

He rushed over to the Corporal and tried to lift the ramp that was crushed down onto Hall's chest. His body armour was all that had stopped his body from being flattened. Taylor tried with all his strength, but the exosuit was not enough. The ramp had fixed solid on its mountings to the wrecked enemy fighter. Without another word, the two creatures stepped up, and one gently pushed Taylor aside. Hall could only watch in amazement as they took hold of the wreckage, hauled it from his body and out the way, before dropping it with a heavy crash to the deck.

Footsteps hammered into the docking bay, and Parker

was at the head of her platoon. Taylor leapt up to stand in front of the creatures.

"Wait!" he shouted.

Eli stopped in shock, but none of them dared defy the Major's orders.

"Demiran's gone, but these two are with us!"

"What you mean 'with us'? They're the enemy!"

"I don't have time to explain. All you need know is that these two soldiers just saved my life and that of Corporal Hall."

"They're the reason you're down here and nearly died in the first place!"

"Sergeant! This is not up for discussion!"

He turned back to the two creatures. They were helping Hall get to his feet in a scene that touched them all. They were not sure whether to believe the sincerity of the creatures or not, but they were all amazed to have found Taylor alive, that they were willing to entertain the idea while it lasted.

"The station is overrun, and we have to get back to our command centre. Have you got weapons, and are you willing to use them to fight alongside us?"

The two creatures both nodded in agreement.

"Mitch, if Demiran is gone, what hope do we have?"

"Not much, but I will not sit back and wait to die. Let's get back to Kelly, and make sure we give the Commander every chance he has to hold onto this God damn station!"

CHAPTER ELEVEN

Taylor strode briskly down the halls of the station with Parker and Hall one side and the two aliens on his other flank. They wore more sleek and embellished armour than the typical Mechs and were clearly something special. Taylor knew they were guards to an important enemy leader and were certainly an entirely different quality of soldier to the hulking infantry they were used to fighting.

As they passed a corridor of Mechs, the two alien allies opened fire and struck down two of the Mechs as they passed. Parker watched in amazement. None of them knew yet whether they could be trusted or not. The aliens seemed to have such little regard for life that he wondered if killing their own would bother them at all. Taylor reached a comms unit and quickly patched into the CP.

"This is Taylor, we're en route. What is the current situation?"

"Major, we're in deep shit! Jones is trapped in an office near 71A. Achen has dug in outside the CP, and no word from Nichols. Chen is falling back here also."

Taylor could hear the screams of scores of wounded all around on the other end of the line.

"Jones? Is he still alive?"

"Last we heard, yes, but I've lost the feeds from the area, and we can't reach him."

"Alright, we'll do what we can to assist the Captain."

"Major?"

"What is it?"

"A small enemy craft attempted to leave the station just a few minutes ago."

Taylor's eyes lit up. *Demiran, you bastard!*

"Did it escape?"

"Its engines were hit by our fighters, and the last I saw it was spinning out of control."

Taylor smiled. "Good to know, Lieutenant, over and out."

Taylor turned back to the troops, but Eli interrupted him before he could speak.

"Why didn't you tell him it was Demiran?"

"Not on an open channel, Sergeant. If his ship went out of control, then there's a good chance he won't get picked up for some time. We might have just bought ourselves a little extra time. Until he can contact his forces, they will assume we still have him."

He turned to the others.

"Jones is in trouble, and the rest of our forces have fallen back to the CP. I will not leave our people out there. Let's move!"

Taylor leapt forward and the two aliens were the first to follow after him. He still found it hard to fathom that they were at his side, but he'd take any help he could get when they were on their knees and fighting for their survival.

Ten minutes later, they were close enough to hear the fire ahead. Taylor stopped quickly to survey a map of the area that was on one of the walls. He peaked around the corner of his position to see the enemy forces still pouring into the office district, and fire from Reitech weapons was flowing through the breach.

"Alright, no time for subtleties. Jones might not have long. Parker, I want you to take half the troops down this parallel corridor. Engage the enemy at your first opportunity."

She turned and signalled for fifteen of the soldiers to follow her before leaping across the crossroads to take the next route as Taylor had ordered. He looked back to see that Hall and the aliens were at his back. It still sent his pulse racing every time he turned back to see the aliens just centimetres from his face.

"Let's move."

They rushed out from the corridor and sprinted towards their target. Seven of the Mechs were visible at the entrance to the office, and the others were already inside. Pulses from the two creatures running beside him joined Taylor's fire. They kept up the pace as they butchered the creatures. When they had made half the distance, their fire was met with Parker's as her troops smashed the enemy ahead of them.

Taylor did not stop when his magazine ran dry. He drew his Assegai and screamed a battle cry and continued rushing forward under the cover of friendly guns. He leapt onto the nearest Mech that had already been reduced to its knees and thrust his weapon into its torso, running it up to the hilt.

The two alien allies reached his side and tore into the remaining Mechs. They fought with a nimbleness that he had only seen in Karadag. He was left speechless as they ripped apart four of the soldiers with their bare hands. Taylor sheathed his weapon and slammed his back up against the doorway for cover, slipping a new magazine into his rifle.

The room had gone silent with both sides in shock and surprise. They knew there were still a sizeable number of creatures the other side of the door; and between them and Jones' troops.

"Jones!" called Taylor.

The Captain's ears pricked up in surprise.

"Jones!" he repeated. "We've come to get you out of here! Watch your fire!"

"You've got a clean angle!" he shouted back.

Taylor took his opportunity and leapt around the corner into the broad open doorway. The Mechs fumbled to try and re-direct towards him but came under fire from Jones' position as Taylor opened fire. Parker and the others jumped to his aid, and their enemy was caught in a brutal crossfire. A few seconds later, and there was nothing left standing of the enemy force. Their bodies lined the floor, and smoke arose from the burning pulses of Taylor's newest allies.

Jones arose from his position, and several of his platoon were helping the wounded to their feet. The Captain approached and looked at the two aliens standing beside Taylor in disbelief. He had already realised they were fighting alongside the Major, but he could not help but stare. He trusted Taylor's judgement and so let it be.

"Heard you were in the shit," said Taylor.

"Aren't we all?" replied Jones.

"Everywhere is in a complete mess. All we know for sure is Kelly still holds the CP. We are to retreat to his position and hold."

Jones knew he was trading one desperate situation for another, but he was glad to at least be back on his feet and not huddled down in a corner. Taylor turned to see the two aliens looked down at their fallen kin with some curiosity, but they appeared to show no sadness for their deaths. He turned and led the troops without a single word.

It took them fifteen minutes to reach the CP as they worked their way through corridors filled with debris and the dead from both sides. As they approached Kelly's position, they heard cheers ring out and stopped as they heard the trampling of heavy steps. He lifted his hand to stop and then turned and whispered for them to take up positions.

A few seconds later, a dozen Mechs took the bend up ahead and were running at a sizeable pace away from the CP. Taylor ducked down at the first sight of them, expecting some new attack, but then he realised; they were running away.

"Now!" he ordered.

He lifted himself up and opened fire, basking in the bloodshed around him. He'd not let them escape to fight them again in another hour or another day. A few of the creatures tried to raise their weapons and fight, taking cover in the edges of the hallway, but they didn't stand a chance.

Taylor had for a long time wondered how it felt so emotionless to kill the enemy, even something to enjoy. He knew he would never feel this way if they had been human, and yet the aliens were feeling more human as every day went by. The two aliens stood at his side, and fighting with him only made that feeling stronger. He stopped firing and turned to look at their faces; and watched to see that they were engulfed in the slaughter as

Hall and Parker beside them.

Before the last body had hit the ground, Taylor was stepping over the body of the first. He was striding quickly towards the CP, and the yells and shouts of excitement and celebration were growing louder. They reached the atrium that led to the Command Centre and found Major Achen stood there.

"Whoa, hang on! What the hell are they doing with weapons?"

He was gesturing towards the two aliens behind the Major and had his rifle ready to use.

"They're with me. Get used to it."

Taylor tried to step past, but Achen mirrored him and continued to block his entry.

"You may go to the Commander, but they stay here!"

Taylor shrugged his shoulders and accepted that the Major was right. He turned back to Eli.

"Sergeant, hold here. Take up defensive positions, and be sure nobody picks a fight with our new friends."

Achen stepped aside and let Taylor pass. He stepped through into the CP to see it was littered with casualties, but many of them smiled through their pain and celebrated with the others who were still standing. Kelly turned form the comms desk with a huge grin spanning across his face.

"Schulz has arrived! The enemy is in full retreat!"

"I thought he didn't have much in the way of combat ships?"

"They don't know that, do they?"

Taylor strode forward with a laugh and shook Kelly's hand in friendship.

"We made it, Major. You did it."

"I didn't get Demiran, Sir."

Kelly looked puzzled.

"His craft was hit leaving the station and was last seen out of control and heading far away."

Kelly smiled. "Good, we got rid of the bastard and survived, all in one. General Schulz is coming aboard imminently, and your presence is required at Docking Bay Charlie. You've got ten minutes."

Taylor turned and quickly made his way back to his troops who were waiting uncomfortably outside. Parker was sat against a sidewall and staring at the two aliens. He panned around the atrium and could see that most of the humans glared at them and kept weapons close to hand. The creatures stood in a relaxed fashion with their visors still back, and their heads bare for all to see. Mitch couldn't have believed he could ever trust one of the aliens in anyway, let alone with his life, but he knew he was alive because of them. He stepped up to their position. They towered a good half metre over him.

"What are your names?"

The two creatures look at him in surprise, as if it was the last thing they had expected in the world.

"Our leaders use no names for us."

"What do you mean?" he asked.

The other stepped forward and answered.

"Names in public are for Lords and those wealthy enough to deserve it."

Taylor had always thought of them as a faceless enemy, and yet he never realised how close he was to be correct.

"Jesus Christ," replied Jones.

Taylor looked back at them and felt some pity for how they lived.

"You must have names which you use for each other?"

They nodded in agreement.

"Then I would know your names, and they shall be used from this day forth."

"Then I am Jafar, and this is Tsengal."

"Alright, I am Major Mitch Taylor, and from now on you are serving with the 2nd Inter-Allied Battalion under the command of Colonel Chandra. I am her second in command."

Chandra stepped into the room as he spoke and heard her name, but she was too shocked at the sight of the two aliens to ask for clarification. She'd heard about their presence from others in their Company, but she hadn't believed it until now. As obscure a situation as it was, she could see Taylor trusted them, and that was enough for her. She stepped forward to involve herself in the conversation.

"I hear you saved Taylor's life?"

"Only after he had saved ours," replied Jafar.

"You have given yourself to his service, but will you follow me? Will you fight for Earth, and abide by our chain of command? I will not, and cannot, have anyone in this unit who is not here to fight for everyone amongst us."

"We are at your will. All we ask is the opportunity to fight beside you."

She sighed as she thought about their proposal. It was the first she'd ever spoken to one of the creatures, and it scarcely seemed believable what they were asking. Yet she looked into their eyes and could see they were not so different to a human. It was a culture clash, and just as she'd had many times back home in previous years.

"Your support is appreciated. You must expect that your presence amongst us will come as a shock to many, and you will not be accepted lightly. Continue to prove yourselves and fight for our cause, and you'll be well on your way. One thing is for certain, you can't stay looking like that."

They looked down at their armour and then to the troops all around them. Their blackened armour and bloody red ornamentation was in stark contrast to the human forces. She reached forward and tapped the armour. It felt like the armour of a tank.

"Sergeant Silva!"

He rushed to her position.

"Yes, Ma'am!"

"These boys are joining us. I want them in uniform."

The Sergeant looked puzzled for a moment.

"Vehicles paints. Get them sprayed up to match our disruptive patterns, and whack some insignia on them. They're in this Battalion now."

"Yes, Ma'am!" he replied.

He turned to the two creatures. The hulking Sergeant was used to towering over all those under his command, but the huge creatures belittled the proud man. He had to look up to make eye contact.

"Follow me!"

"Schulz is arriving any minute, and we should be there," said Taylor.

"Christ, nobody mentioned it, let's move!"

* * *

The two entered the docking bay just as Schulz's shuttle was on an approach to land. Taylor could see Eddie lying about on a storage crate to their side.

"Rains! You survived, you son of a bitch!" Taylor called over to him.

Eddie turned with a pained smile but was clearly exhausted.

"Kato make it?"

"He's with the medics, right now. Hurt bad, but I think he'll make it."

"Good."

"More than I can say for my new gal."

Taylor looked puzzled.

Eddie nodded and gestured towards the wreck of a copter. There were several holes in the fuselage, the cockpit was smashed, and half of the undercarriage was destroyed. Taylor shook his head.

"How on Earth did you get out of that? Better still, how did you even land it?"

"She's my gal. She was always gonna get me through this."

"Pipe down!" a shout came out from one of the officers who had arrived ahead of Schulz to welcome him. Taylor turned in scorn to glare at the officer who stood triumphantly on the docking bay as if he'd won the battle, when in reality, he'd only arrived a few minutes ago.

The shuttle came to a smooth landing, and Schulz was first out of the door to a roar of excitement and cheering. Taylor wondered why anyone bothered, or was it just expected? Few of the Inter-Allied there showed any emotion at all besides being a little bored.

General Schulz quickly made his greetings to Kelly and the other officers, and then headed right for Taylor, ignoring Chandra who stood at his side.

"I hear you have two of the enemy elite troops, bodyguards of one of their leaders? Well done, you must have them transferred to the MPs immediately. They could be very useful."

Schulz tried to turn and leave before Taylor could utter a word, but he was forced to stop upon the Major's response.

"Negative, Sir. They stay with us."

The General glared at him in astonishment, but he also knew he must be more careful with Taylor than their previous confrontation in France. He opened his mouth to speak, but Taylor jumped in before any words were spoken.

"They have already been welcomed into the Inter-Allied and have proven their worth among us. They fight with us, and they stay with us."

Schulz wasn't sure whether he was more surprised at Taylor's insubordination once again, or the fact that he was defending alien forces.

"Are you trying to tell me they are fighting by your side against their own?"

"Yes, Sir."

Chandra interrupted as she could see the situation was going sour.

"They not only saved two officers' lives, but proved invaluable in the defence of this station, Sir."

Schulz thought about it for just a moment, leaning in close to Taylor so that his entourage could not hear.

"While you keep fighting and getting results, you've got a certain leeway, Major, but make no mistake, this is on you. If they fuck up, if they kill our own, or if they compromise a mission in anyway, it's your balls on the line."

Schulz leaned back and smiled as he looked into Taylor's eyes with arrogance.

"Always is, Sir," replied Taylor.

Mitch thought they had overcome at least some of their differences, but Schulz appeared to be back to his usual unlikeable self.

It could be worse, thought Taylor.

The General continued on until he reached a small podium that had been set up for him so that he could address the gathered crowd. Most had fought the initial attack and defence of the station, but those who hadn't, stood out like a sore thumb with their pristine uniforms.

"Today we took the first step in reclaiming our solar system. Earth is ours once more, but we will not stop until this solar system is totally ours once again. It'll be another eight hours until we can get the rest of our forces ferried here. Until that time, I want you to take some rest, and ready yourselves for tomorrow. For tomorrow, we go to the Moon and drive the alien bastards from the colony that rightly belongs in human hands!"

Clapping echoed around the spacious docking bay until Schulz called it to a close.

"I want all command staff to meet in thirty minutes in the newly established CP at Hall 2B, floor six. From there, we can thrash out our intentions for tomorrow. Have your troops rest easy, but I want watches set by all units throughout our stay here. Thank you all."

Thirty minutes later, Taylor and Chandra stood alongside more than thirty other officers as Schulz hashed out his plan. It was simple, but there seemed no other options.

"I know this isn't the most complex plan in the world, but we have little intelligence to go on. However, we have Commander Kelly along, and he and his people are intimately familiar with their former homeland. We strike the Lunar colony with everything we have. We use overwhelming force and strength of number to bring this battle to a close. By tomorrow evening, we'll either be celebrating our victory or heading for Earth with our tail between our legs. The latter is not an option!"

"Sir, the Parliament building?" asked Kelly.

Schulz nodded in agreement.

"Yes. Commander Kelly has rightfully asked for the honour of re-taking the administrative capitol. However, he will need an additional battalion to support his efforts, do I have a volunteer?"

Taylor turned to ask Chandra, but her hand was already raised. It sent a shiver down his spine to know she was right there with him.

"We'll do it, Sir."

Schulz looked quickly at Chandra and then straight on

to Taylor. He was surprised the Major did not voice any objection.

"Commander?" he asked Kelly.

"It'd be an honour to have the Inter-Allied covering our backs."

"Alright, Inter-Allied will breach here, half a kilometre west of Kelly's forces, and they will encircle the Parliament buildings. They may not mean much to our enemy, but to our people they are vital. You all know what you have to do. You have until 0800 hours. Catch some rest."

Chatter rang out throughout the room as the officers dispersed. Kelly quickly pushed through them to catch Taylor on the way out of the CP.

"Major, may I have a word for a moment?"

Taylor turned back to Chandra for clarification.

"It's alright, I'll see you back at our post in a little while."

Taylor followed the Commander around a corner to a quiet spot. Kelly didn't appear to present any threat to him, but curiosity made Taylor's mind run wild with what he might have to say. They were finally out of earshot of the passing troops, and he whispered carefully.

"When you hunted Demiran down, I know Lieutenant Perera was involved too. I know you both got to that docking bay, and I know he didn't make it out alive. I also know his actions earlier were counterproductive to our operations and insubordinate."

Taylor sighed and tried to answer, but Kelly cut him

short.

"Perera hated you. We both know it. All I want to know is if his death could have been avoided. Are you a man I can trust, and are you the man that your reputation would imply?"

"I hope so, Sir. Perera did not die at my hands, but only because I was unable to defend myself in that moment. He'd have gunned me down, there and then."

"Then I am sorry. Sorry that one of my own could do such a thing. Please let us put this all behind us. You have already convinced me of your worth. Pull this mission off, and you will gain the respect of my people."

"I wasn't looking for it, Sir. I never have. I have tried to do everything I can in this war and continue to do so. If people don't like me, that's their problem, not mine."

Kelly smiled. "You're a true warrior, Major. I am only glad you are on our side."

Kelly turned and left Taylor. He was glad of the Commander's support. He'd almost been stabbed in the back once that day, and the last thing he needed were enemies on his own side.

Taylor got back to their billets for the day. They'd had been allocated a sports facility, consisting mostly of open halls and with little furniture. Many of the troops had already set up their beds and were relaxing, playing cards, or chatting with their comrades. He was glad to see that the newly enlisted troops to Inter-Allied were mingling with the hardened veterans as if they'd never been apart. Chandra was busy looking over her Mappad when he strode up to her. She looked up with a grim expression.

"Final casualties for us, thirty-three dead. Twenty-eight wounded."

"It could have been a lot worse," he replied.

"I wonder when this is all over if this will even resemble the unit we started in any way."

"We're still here, aren't we?"

She nodded in agreement. "For now."

Taylor could see that the Colonel was sitting amongst her own gear and in the same room as the rest. There were no luxuries afforded the officers that day.

"All this worry for our own good, and you volunteered us to assist Kelly without a moment's thought?"

"It didn't need any further thought. We're going to the Moon tomorrow, whether we want to or not. If we're at the centre of the assault, it'll boost the morale of all who join us. We also need this bitter animosity resolved between your marines and the Lunar colonists. It's almost led to your incarceration and death, and maybe you won't be so lucky a third time."

Taylor hunkered down and took a seat on Chandra's bed beside her.

"You know we need to promote Grey before this mission is over. He's proven more than capable, and as a Company commander, he needs greater authority. And let's not forget, when Suarez returns, we want the better man in command."

"Where is the Lieutenant? I haven't seen him since a few days after we reached Paris," asked Chandra.

Taylor laughed at the idea that she hadn't even noticed his absence.

"General White wanted a volunteer to head back to the US and assist with the training of newly enlisted troops. He thought one of the Immortals could do wonders for recruiting and training."

"And you sent them Suarez?"

"Hey, I did exactly what was asked. I wasn't about to give up anymore than I had to."

She nodded in agreement.

"How did he ever come to be an officer in your marines? He's selfish, confrontational, and obnoxious. I'd not want to trust my life in his hands."

"No, and yet he's been with us through the worst of it all. I don't like him, but I will not dismiss his efforts. Suarez certainly pulled some strings to get where he did, but can you blame him?"

They both fell silent for a few moments as they watched the troops who had quickly made the halls their home. They could see fatigue in many of the faces, but they were as steadfast as ever.

"You've got until morning to rest. I suggest you make good use of that time," Chandra said.

"Morning? If I didn't have a watch, I'd never have known night from day here. Remind me to never take a posting off of Earth in the future. There ain't much to like about it."

"Agreed, and yet thousands of people think otherwise."

"God knows why."

Taylor sighed as he pulled himself to his feet and stepped over to where Parker had set up her gear and erected Taylor's bed next to hers. He wearily unclipped the harness of his exosuit and webbing, dropping it down to the floor. He stretched and felt immense relief to have the weight and bulk off his shoulders. He turned to see that Jafar and Tsengal were sat against a wall just a few metres from their position. The two aliens were silent. He had not noticed them immediately, for they now sported camouflage paint and Inter-Allied insignia. They both remained quiet and seemed to be studying everything around them.

Parker kept a keen eye on the two aliens, and Taylor could tell that it was the most uncomfortable thing he had ever done, allowing them to become one of them. He wanted to explain to her how they had saved his life, but he knew he had to be careful who knew about that turn of events. He turned and looked to Jafar and Tsengal.

"How do you like your new look?"

They peered down at their camouflaged suits that still shone from the fresh paint, even though it was a perfect matt finish. They seemed overwhelmed by all that was happening to them but far from uncomfortable. Taylor got up and staggered over to their position and took a knee.

"I can't make you one of them overnight, but bit by bit, you will become one of us. Tomorrow we go into combat once again. Will you join us? Will you help us take back the Lunar colony?"

"Whatever you ask of us," replied Jafar.

Taylor shook his head.

"No, I am not your master. I am one of your officers, but I want to know how you feel about it."

Tsengal looked confused.

"Why would you ask us? What does it matter?"

"Because while I may be in charge of all, bar the Colonel around here, I value the opinions of my troops."

The two still looked puzzled but also quite impressed by his sentiment.

"Now tell me something. You speak our language as if you always knew it. How is that possible?"

"From when we are born, we are inserted with a chip in our brains. It works as a subconscious translator so that we can speak and listen in any language. New languages can be learnt within a few hours of reading or hearing them. I am surprised your race have nothing similar when you have many languages, like our people."

Taylor shook his head in disbelief.

"Fascinating, but we've not got anything like it."

He thought back to Schulz who wanted them sent back as lab rats.

"Many of our leaders would have you sent back to our homeland for interrogation and experimentation. I promise you, I will not let that happen while you remain members of this Battalion and continue to give everything you have to fight for it."

"You have our allegiance."

"I ask a lot of you, what do you ask in return?"

Once again the two creatures looked surprised that they were asked their opinion.

"Only to be one of you. You have shown us what life could be like, and we want what you have."

Taylor smiled. Their lives had been hell since the war began, and yet here were two from the other side who would give everything for the same.

"Your weapons, food, everything else, can you organise your own?"

"There is enough lying about this station from the battle which we can salvage," replied Tsengal.

"Alright, then go and get what you need, but do not go anywhere without human members of this unit. Others might not be so accepting of you, nor believe your participation in this army. Find Corporal Hall, and join him in his watch at 1100 hours."

Taylor got to his feet and finally wandered over to join

Parker for good. She was clearly still uneasy about his friendship with the two aliens, but she was warmed by his presence.

It wasn't long before he lay down to rest his weary body in readiness for the morning assault. Eli lay down in her own bed that was pushed up to his. Their hands were intertwined, and they remained silent, reflecting on the day's events. She broke the silence between them, but it was still quiet enough for only Taylor to hear over the chatter in the vast room.

"Tomorrow, all this could be over. The last human colony back in our hands."

Taylor smiled. He wished it could be true, but he knew in his gut that it couldn't be.

"Still a few stations to take, and God knows what state Mars is in."

"Who cares about Mars? It was nothing but a crappy research centre anyway."

"Can't say I have any interest in it either, but our job is to eradicate the enemy presence from the entire solar system."

"Mmm."

He turned at her expression.

"Makes you wonder where they have come from. How they found us, and what other life they have found and tried to utterly destroy?"

"Why don't you ask Jafar and Tsengal? I'm sure they

could answer some of your questions."

She sighed. It was clear she had no intention of ever speaking to them, let alone trusting anything they had to say.

"There are many times in our history when an enemy one day, or one year, is an ally the next."

"But those were humans, our own people. We always had something in common with them."

"I am sure that is not the way the native Indians felt, nor the Africans under British rule, or the Mayans when the Spanish invaded. So they look different and come from different lands. I've seen more humanity in those two than some of the spineless bastards we've had to deal with back home."

They eventually fell asleep that night, and Taylor got the best sleep he'd had all year; surrounded by his companions, and awaiting a mission which would reclaim the ground that was the one blemish on his career and conscience. He was up early and before most of the others. Only Chandra was fully awake and already geared up.

"Another day, another fight, hey, Colonel," Taylor said.

An hour later, they were formed up at their docking bay as agreed. Rains stood beside a newly arrived copter while the wreck of his old one still lay untouched in the docking bay deck. The area was silent, and they were all awaiting the final command by Schulz. Finally, his voice came over the tannoy.

"Good morning to you all. Today we embark on a mission to re-claim a colony which had long been lost to the enemy. We stand ten thousand strong, and the Moon Defence forces, that fought so bravely to defend their lands, are among us today. We fight for them, for their homes and lands. But we also fight for our own. The Moon was the first civilian colony to be attacked, and they fought bravely. Let us honour their sacrifices here today, and reclaim it in the name of the human race!"

Cheers rang out. Inter-Allied shared their docking bay with Kelly's MDF forces and another thousand troops. The deck below them shook under the stamping of feet from the excitement of the troops.

"Yesterday, we lost many fine soldiers to capture this station, and many more will bear scars and wounds for life. Let us remember them, and honour their efforts today by continuing their fine work. Good luck, and God speed. COs have your troops emplane. The time has come for us to strive forward and seek victory!"

The crowds cheered once again and many of the Inter-Allied troops could not help but join in. Taylor was impressed, despite not wanting to be. He never disliked Schulz as a leader, only as a man.

CHAPTER TWELVE

The fleet was rapidly descending on the Lunar colony, and the troops sat quietly aboard next to the copters. Taylor and Chandra were aboard the Deveron once again. It had been hastily patched up after the last battle. As infantry, they all prayed they would make it to land intact, for there was nothing they could do until that time.

The Colonel and Eli sat one side of Taylor, Jafar and Tsengal the other. Captain Jones sat opposite them. It suddenly struck Taylor how accepting the Captain had been of their new allies, especially when he thought back to the punishment and suffering he had faced at the aliens' hands. Taylor nodded at him and gestured for him to leave their seats for a word. The two officers stepped out of the landing bays and out of sight of the others.

"I have brought two creatures into our unit. Creatures which until recently fought against us. It's not been a popular move, and yet you're one of the few who doesn't seem to have had a problem with it. It surprises me. You've got more reason than any of them to hate these newcomers."

Jones shrugged his shoulders as if he had nothing to add.

"Come on, Charlie, I need you with me a hundred percent, and that means I need to know what you're thinking."

Jones looked down and then back up at Taylor. There was sadness in his eyes that Taylor had awoken.

"They may have done some horrific things to me, but it wasn't those two. The two out there are soldiers, just like us. I'd like to think if I were ever captured that I would be treated the way you treat prisoners."

"But you weren't."

"No, but that's no reason to act like animals. I have chosen to base my judgement on Jafar and Tsengal on what I see with my own eyes, not what we think of them based on some reputation. You say they saved your life. They certainly helped saved mine. As far as I am concerned, they are our comrades, providing they continue on as they have started."

Taylor smiled in response.

"You've come a long way since those dark days, back to the man I used to know."

"Mostly," he replied.

Lieutenant Ryan came over the intercom.

"We're on approach to the colony, all troops to board their copters. Clear the decks, and gunners to their positions. May God be with you all."

"God? I wasn't aware he was watching," replied Taylor.

Taylor laughed. "Let's go."

Fifteen minutes later, the Deveron's guns opened fire on the enemy ships approaching their positions. They expected a vicious defence and knew that the battle must have commenced a good fifteen minutes before their arrival as the first wave of fighters and cruisers tried to cut a path through.

Taylor was strapped in aboard Rains' copter when the first enemy pulse smashed into the Deveron. The ship rocked violently but continued onwards. They could just hear the sound of Ryan's orders echoing around the docking bay outside.

"Docking doors open, launch in five, four, three..."

The engines roared to life around them, and a second later their craft rushed out from the Deveron's docking bays; out into space where railgun rounds and pulses flashed past the windows of their craft.

"Jesus Christ!" Hall shouted.

"Hold on to your asses, this is gonna be a rough one!" replied Eddie.

Their copter dodged and evaded pulses and the wreckage of fighters from both sides as it soared towards the Moon. All around they watched ships of both sides interlocked into dogfights. Beyond them, they could see the larger ships duking it out and tearing each other apart. The Deveron was long out of sight, but they knew Ryan would have taken them quickly forward into the battle.

Taylor and Chandra were closest to the cockpit and could see the Moon looming ahead of them. Pulses rushed towards them from ground positions, and they could only watch in horror as one of the MDF copters burst into pieces as it took a direct hit.

"Still happy you volunteered to go in with Kelly?" called Taylor.

She turned and glared at him. They both knew it was the right course of action, but they only hoped they could survive long enough to reach the surface. A minute later that felt like five, they were banking hard and coming in to land. Chandra blew a sigh of relief as she realised they had passed within the enemy's defence grid.

"Now it's on us!" shouted Taylor.

It had been a long time since Taylor had set foot on the Lunar colony, and it was a wound that still cut deep in that they'd had to flee from it so quickly. He was eager to make up for the orders he'd never wished to receive; finally he was given the opportunity.

"Half of you were with me when we came here last, and remember that day! Because today we get payback!"

Eddie brought them in for a rapid landing. They hit the

ground hard, to the level that the undercarriage buckled slightly as they put down. The troops were quickly on their feet and heading for the door. Taylor smashed his hand down onto the door release, and they were out into the low gravity of the Moon.

"Head for that door!" Chandra ordered.

Taylor turned to see a main access point into the station. They had landed exactly on target as Kelly had asked. He leapt from the door and bounced along the surface towards the several metres wide entrance. It looked as if it was intended for more than one vehicle to pass through at a time, and there was a numeric datapad for entry on the wall. Taylor punched in the code Kelly had given him, and the huge doors quickly lifted. The structure looked thick enough to withstand heavy artillery.

The Major looked back to see that the other copters had all landed bar one which was missing. It was relatively few losses, considering the vicious assault, but still many friends lost. They had half the Battalion with them, Jones having led the rest to an entrance a few hundred metres away.

He turned and rushed inside the facility. Within five minutes, the doors were once again shut and all were inside. Gravity had returned to normal as the doors clamped down, but the air was still thin. They were all aware that breaches in the facility meant that there was too little air to go without their helmets.

They had entered what was a vehicle depot for land based craft, but it was littered with heavily damaged enemy craft.

"Looks like a salvage yard," Taylor said.

"They must have been using this place to reassemble what they could from parts," replied Chandra.

"Seems a little desperate," he replied.

"Good, it's a sign of the times. They must be running pretty thin."

Their communications were down once again. They all looked forward to the day their tech guys could find a way around the jamming, but for now they were on their own. The troops waited patiently for Chandra, and it made the room almost silent. They suspected much of the fighting had already started, but they were almost half a kilometre from the nearest allied troops.

"Why haven't we met any resistance yet?" asked Chandra.

Taylor shrugged his shoulders. They all hoped there was a good reason for it, but it seemed too easy. She stood up and signalled for them to follow her. There were two exits from the room into the nearby corridors. She signalled for Jackson to take the far side, and she continued onwards with Taylor and Lieutenant Ota's Company.

Mitch got ahead of Chandra and led from the front. He reached the doorway and peered through the Perspex plate in the centre and turned to shake his head, confirming there was no contact. He reached for the door switch, and to his surprise it opened. Chandra nodded to Jackson to give the go ahead. They all knew that from now on they only had one goal.

"Go!" she whispered.

Taylor leapt forward and charged through the doorway into the broad corridor. As he did so, he heard the clatter of feet moving quickly and approaching from the west side. He turned back and ushered through a dozen of the troops, ducked down into position, and signalled for Chandra to stop where she was. They waited anxiously as the sound grew louder, and it became quickly apparent it was a dozen Mechs rushing towards them. Mitch nodded and held up three fingers to count down as they approached.

Mitch quickly made the count, lifting himself up as the last finger dropped, and opened fire. He continued to shoot in rapid succession. The creatures seemed to be caught completely unawares by their presence. In just five seconds, they were cut to pieces and only managed to get off a few frantic shots against the hastily prepared ambush. Taylor got to his feet and wandered over to check the bodies. Jafar appeared next to him and carefully studied the fallen creatures.

Taylor had never assigned the two aliens to a platoon or company. He knew he could not trust his own people with them yet. As a result, they kept close to him and the

Colonel at all times; a fact that made many uncomfortable.

"117th, they were amongst the first to land on Earth. I believe they fought in Spain and were near Paris towards the end of the war."

"End? This war never ended," said Taylor.

"He's right," Chandra agreed. "It did end, the war for Earth ended. But we are in a new conflict now, and something humanity has never seen before."

"These troops have little ammunition between them. They look malnourished, and many have wounds that are not fully healed," continued Jafar.

"What are you suggesting?" she asked.

"That these are battle weary troops. Soldiers that are on the run from a war already lost," replied Taylor.

Chandra looked quickly over to Jafar.

"Is that what you would draw from this?"

The alien nodded in agreement.

"The base ship is nowhere to be seen. The fact we managed to land without opposition tells me they are spread thin. The last I heard was that our leaders, our former leaders, were losing heart and looking to end this campaign."

"Why did you not tell us this sooner?" asked Chandra.

"It is just rumour, Ma'am. We never knew much but what we were ordered."

"Alright, well I hope you're right. Jackson should hopefully be making good progress, so let's be sure to keep up."

They turned and continued on throughout the vast access tunnel. It was broad enough for them to walk twelve wide and with a sizeable space between each other. They made it a hundred metres without any contact of any kind when Chandra broke the silence.

"You really believe what he is saying?"

"I think there's a damn good chance, yes. It's not winning this battle that concerns me, for I know we can. It's what we may have to face after it."

They took a bend up ahead and the corridor lit up as five pulses rushed towards them. Taylor leapt aside, shoving Chandra out of harm's way. They both tumbled aside and landed hard against the metal interior.

"Guess they aren't quite finished yet!" she yelled.

The pulses died down after a moment, and the Colonel leant around just enough to get a view of what they faced.

"Fuck, I can see at least twenty Mechs dug in."

"Then we take the tunnels."

Chandra looked back at Taylor with her eyes wide open.

"I know you don't like it, but Kelly and his people made good use of them."

"Bullshit, we don't have time."

She looked back at the enemy defences that were a hundred metres around the corner. She turned back to the troops.

"Hall! Get me a runner! Tell Jackson to swing around

our way and give us a hand!"

"Yes, Ma'am!"

They sent the runner and waited out for five minutes. Chandra grew impatient, and she stood up tall and bellowed her orders.

"Up! Now! We've got a job to do. Everyone is relying on us to get this done rapidly. Any delay and we risk the entire mission! Ready your weapons, and be ready on my go!"

"What are you doing?" Taylor demanded.

"We have superior numbers and firepower but limited time. We can take this position with a frontal assault."

"Frontal assault?" he responded in shock.

"We have no choice. Let's get in there and do our jobs!"

Taylor edged around to the corner and could see there was no cover down the long spartan corridor.

"God damn, we could have used the shields for this!"

"Well, when Reiter finishes his changes, and gets them back to us, you'll be the first to have one," replied Chandra.

She got up and beckoned for the troops near her to come in close.

"This plan relies on speed. We must overcome that position with all haste. We have enough numbers that a quick rush could overwhelm them with minimal casualties. Are you with me?"

She could see that none were keen, but they all nodded in agreement.

"Alright, ready yourselves, on three. We do not stop until this is over. Three, two, one!"

Chandra leapt out into the corridor, and another dozen of their troops were in the corridor when she'd fired off her first round. Just as she pulled the trigger, the first two pulses rushed down the corridor, narrowly missing them all. They knew they would not be so lucky a second time. They flooded into the tunnel as ordered, and those at the front fired rapidly to try and give some cover.

Chandra gasped as the Mechs ahead lifted a heavy weapon up onto the barricade and were about to fire when their position was lit up by gunfire, and shots echoed out from the other side of their position. The heavy weapon team quickly abandoned their weapon and turned to take on a new threat.

"This is our chance!" she shouted.

They were already running, but she and Taylor increased to a sprint, and their suits allowed a rapid pace to cover the distance. They leapt up onto the defensive line to find only two Mechs still alive and fighting. They blasted them from their high position and looked up to see their saviours. Captain Jackson stood at the head of his Company with the barrel of his gun smoking violently.

"Hell of a good timing there, Captain," Chandra said.

He didn't respond but only marvelled at his work.

Taylor was relieved as he looked around to see only one of theirs had been clipped on the way in but was still breathing. He look to Chandra and shook his head in disbelief.

"Alright, let's move on."

They readied their weapons and continued on as intended. As they closed the distance to the Parliament buildings, they could hear the sound of gunfire. Its intensity rapidly increasing as they grew nearer.

"Kelly must have got there ahead of us, Mitch!" shouted Chandra.

"Then he can't have met much opposition."

Taylor recognised their location and knew they were coming up on the broad atrium that marked the entrance to the Parliament. Kelly had told him of the battle they had fought there when they tried to break out onto the surface months before, and he expected to find it littered with bodies and debris. The hall ahead was opening out to the atrium. They could already make out the shape of a strong defensive position, and dozens of Mechs firing from the top.

"Of all the places they could defend, they chose here?" asked Taylor.

Jafar stepped forward to answer.

"They knew it was strategically important to you. That's makes it important to them."

"Well it looks like Kelly has got stuck in already. If we can bring enough fire to bear on this flank, we should be able to end this."

"There's a balcony overlooking that position just above us." Taylor pointed up.

"Good, take a platoon and get up there, and start laying down some fire ASAP!" Chandra shouted.

Taylor turned back, and the two aliens immediately followed him without hesitation.

"I need a platoon, Lieutenant," he asked of Ota.

She signalled to one of her 2nd Lieutenants.

"This is Sergeant Rios, formerly of the Rangers."

A sergeant leading the platoon and a 2nd Lieutenant in charge of a company, they have taken a beating.

"Follow me," said Taylor.

Mitch led them back to a corridor and then east to a stairway. The two aliens were at the front of the column and still glued to his side. The hulking armoured creatures gave him some comfort, to know that they were on his side. The way up the stairs was quiet.

"We're in luck," he whispered.

They continued quickly on at a quiet jogging pace and up to the next level. Taylor stopped them at the top of the stairs. He was still astonished they had made it without opposition.

"They must be running pretty thin on troops."

"Yes, I'd have expected a much harder fight," Tsengal answered.

"I'm not sure if that's a good thing or not."

They stepped out onto the empty balcony and crept to

the far wall as the battle raged below. They could hear fire now from directly below their feet where Chandra had joined the fight. He pulled himself up just enough to peer over the edge of the small wall he was knelt beside. Mitch smiled as he saw an almost completely clear view of the creatures below. He turned and gestured for the rest of the platoon to join them.

The second the rest of the troop was in position, he shot up to a standing position and threw the barrel of his rifle over the wall.

"Fire!"

The opening volley was almost perfectly in sequence and killed six of the Mechs instantly. A few tried to lift their weapons to respond, but there was little they could do. The automatic fire tore apart the enemy's position. He could hear a few of the Rangers shouting insults as they blazed away, but there was too much noise from the intense fire to understand what they said.

Muzzle flashes lit up below them as the troops on the level below rushed up to the enemy positions and jumped up onto the enemy wall to join in the slaughter. Even after all the Mechs were dead, they continued to fire into them, enjoying the utter destruction of their foes.

"Hold fire!" Taylor ordered.

A few moments later the Commander leapt into the middle of the bloodshed and looked up to where Taylor was still surveying the scene. He looked back down at the results of their work and then back up to Taylor with a smile.

"That's some damn fine work, Major!"

Taylor leapt over the wall and used minimal boost to land down on the floor a few metres away from the Commander.

"Sir, I'd have expected a lot more opposition. How are the rest of our forces doing?"

"Last contact we had was from Chen, and it seems it's like this all over."

Taylor shook his head. "I don't like it."

"We are getting our homes back, Major. I'm not going to complain about it being too easy, and I'd like there to be something left by the time this war is over."

Chandra arrived as Kelly finished his last words, and she was about to join the conversation when a call rang out.

"Colonel! Colonel!"

She snapped around at the distraught call. It was Captain Jackson, and he looked panicked.

"Ma'am, we've got incoming. I counted at least a hundred infantry en route."

"Shit, they obviously know where we are and are diverting reinforcements to the breaches," replied Kelly.

"Sir, we'll hold this position. You have to continue on to re-claim this seat of government," Chandra said quietly.

"You sure?"

"We've taken on much worse."

"Alright, Captain Morris, I want all stairs covered. We clear this building one floor at a time!"

Kelly moved away to see to his people, and Chandra turned back to the Inter-Allied troops she had. She looked up to where the Rangers Taylor had led were still watching from the balcony above.

"I want another platoon on that balcony. Ota you can handle that? Captain Jackson, have your troops take up position here. Expand these defences as quickly as you can."

"We'll be packed in pretty tight here," he replied.

"I know, but it's not a bad thing. Nobody is risking explosives here. We need as concentrated fire as we can possibly make. Not a single one of those bastards gets past us!"

"Thank you, Colonel!" Kelly shouted.

He rushed from the scene to continue the sweep through the building. The feeling of taking back what was rightfully theirs overwhelmed him, and he could not help but smile to be home and clawing back their lands, one shot at a time. He led one of the platoons up the nearest staircase and onto the first floor. It was an open plan conference centre. He could see several Mechs step into view to confront them; his smile only widened as he lifted his rifle, and Morris burst into the room on the far side.

* * *

"Come on you bastards!" shouted Chandra, and she fired rapidly into the advancing Mechs.

The creatures were rushing down the hallway up ahead, just as they had done only twenty minutes earlier, but they were meeting a far different defence. Volleys of fire rang out from the fifty troops who had a view of the area, and the lines of creatures were being smashed down. The Mechs continued to pour into the corridor, rushing over their fallen comrades in a desperate bid to take back the Parliament building.

Pulses rushed overhead, and several struck into the defensive wall the enemy themselves had constructed. It was made of some form of resin and seemed almost impervious to the pulses that they fired. Taylor felt the burn of a pulse smash into his position, and it struck Lam with full force. He was thrown back off the wall and onto the floor behind.

Taylor turned, leaping down to check on his comrade, but by the time he'd got to the man, he was already dead. Chandra stepped down to join him. Their attention quickly turned to the eastern perimeter when they realised they didn't have the time to mourn anyone while the battle raged. They rushed over to Jackson's position to find three of his Company dead and five others wounded, but the rest were fighting hard to hold the enemy back. Chandra stepped up to the Captain to look over the defences and could see the creatures pouring into the hallway as far as she could see. She jumped back down next to Taylor as a pulse raced past her head. It melted the edge of her helmet.

"God, they're giving us hell!"

"They must be diverting a lot of their strength to this place. If we can just hold long enough, we could break their armies here," replied Taylor.

"Yes, but we must make sure Kelly succeeds. Take Parker and her section, and go to him. Make sure he raises that flag. It may be vital to our survival!"

Taylor nodded in agreement and rushed off, grabbing Eli from the perimeter. They hurried to the stairway where Kelly had last been seen.

"We need to find the Commander and make sure he gets through this, okay?"

Before they could respond, Jafar and Tsengal stepped up to join them. Taylor could see Eli was as uncomfortable as ever with their presence, but he knew they could be useful.

"Okay, let's do this!"

Taylor quickly followed in Kelly's footsteps. Within a minute, they were in the broad conference hall the Commander had so recently passed through. Over twenty Mechs lay scattered and dead, as well as two MDF soldiers. Another wounded soldier of Kelly's force lay resting against a sidewall with his rifle in hand. A pulse had struck his leg, and he was unable to stand.

"The Commander, where is he?" asked Taylor.

"He carried on to the next floor."

Mitch turned and led his team back to the stairs and up. They were getting further and further from the ground floor and fighting to the extent that it was just a background noise, yet they could still not hear any gunfire from above.

"Kelly must have covered some ground!"

They continued up another three floors until finally they could hear the familiar sound of the Reiter rifles firing rapidly. They reached the floor where the action was taking place and burst out from the stairs to see Kelly up ahead reloading his rifle.

"Kelly!" Taylor shouted.

The Commander slammed in his magazine and quickly lifted his rifle at the sound of his name, but he relaxed when he saw Taylor. Behind him a dozen of his troops continued to battle around a bend on the hallway.

"Where are the rest of your people?"

"We're scattered a little thin, Major. This floor is infested with the bastards!"

"The Colonel is under heavy attack, Sir. We need to turn this around, and we need to show everyone that we have secured this building."

Kelly nodded in agreement. He put down his rifle and

pack and lifted out a flag, the blue and white spot flag of the Lunar colony. He flicked out a telescopic pole and clipped on the flag.

"This second we lift this flag over Parliament, it will change everything. The enemy clearly have eyes on this place."

"Let's do it!"

"On me!" Kelly ordered.

The twelve MDF troops followed Kelly and Taylor's unit to the stairs and continued upwards through the structure. They passed two other floors of fighting where Morris had engaged the enemy. They finally reached the top and rushed out from the stairwell. As they did so, an explosion erupted behind them, and the stairwell collapsed. Taylor turned back in horror to see Parker and the others fall through the breach.

"Eli!" he screamed.

Pulses ripped into their position, and he was suddenly hauled with immense force into a side room. He tumbled in against a desk and looked back to see Jafar had thrown him inside. Only Taylor, Kelly, Jafar and two of the MDF soldiers had made it. Kelly looked horrified and in utter shock.

"We have to go back. We have to go back for them," he muttered.

Taylor gritted his teeth. He wanted to go to Parker's aid more than anything, but he also knew they had a job to do that would save many more lives.

"Sir, this is on us. We have to do this!" Taylor shouted.

"With five soldiers? How?"

"Sir, do you want the Moon back or not? I didn't come here to die!"

He got to his feet and pulled the Commander up.

"How far is it to the roof access?"

Kelly mumbled a little until he regained his composure and could see Taylor was serious.

"It's about fifty metres from here."

"Alright, we have fought our way across a world, a space station, and onto this rock you call a home. We can make it fifty metres!"

He rushed over to a door at the far side and saw a Mech peering through the glass. He quickly lifted his rifle and fired five shots into its head, sending it tumbling to the floor the other side.

"One down!"

He ripped open the door and fired another few shots into the nearest Mech. He looked back to the others with a look of bloodthirsty frenzy. Kelly could see that in that moment, the Major was unstoppable. It gave him a new sense of hope, and he leapt into action, carrying the flag in one hand and lifting his rifle into the other.

The five of them passed quickly through the burnt doorway and over the body of the Mech whose fresh blood spewed out across the hard floor. They got to the end of the hallway when a door beside them burst from its mounts, and the wall at its side it collapsed. Five Mechs burst through into the hall and were already firing before Taylor could respond. The two MDF soldiers were killed instantly, and a pulse smashed into Taylor's rifle that split it in half and continued on to smash into his torso plate.

The power of the pulse launched Taylor into the far wall, and he crumpled down to the ground. He coughed out blood as he turned onto his side. Kelly lifted his rifle, but it was smashed aside by one of the creatures who proceeded to smash a hard strike into his flank. It caused his armour to buckle. It hit him again which launched him down the corridor and onto his back.

Jafar leapt nimbly into action and dodged a pulse and fired rapidly into the first creature. Taylor looked up to see him duck under another strike and thrust a blade into the beast's faceplate that Taylor had not previously seen. He drew his Assegai in one hand and pistol into the other and stumbled to his feet. He rushed forwards firing rapidly. The pistol had a lower calibre version of Reiter's ammunition, but it still needed ten shots to take down the creature.

He jumped onto the next one and thrust down his Assegai into its chest, forcing it to collapse down onto the ground. Just as he drew out the blade, he was hit by the backhand of one of the Mechs and tossed aside. The impact snapped his neck back and broke his right arm. He rolled over on the ground and just managed to get back to his feet. The creature turned its rifle on Taylor and was about to fire when Jafar rushed forwards. He barged it into the wall, and the pulse it fired missed Taylor by just a few centimetres, bursting into the wall behind him.

Taylor marvelled at Jafar's ferocity as he tore the creature's faceplate off and crushed its skull with a single strike. He jumped forward and took his weapon in his left hand as he saw the last reach for Jafar. Mitch thrust his Assegai up into the beast's belly, and it keeled over. He drew the weapon out and thrust it in with two other wicked thrusts to make sure. The two dead Mechs dropped to the floor together.

"You're a formidable fighter," Jafar said.

"Likewise."

Taylor turned as he heard coughing from behind them. Kelly was on his knees but keeled over in immense pain. He rushed over to the Commander who was clearly severely wounded. The flank of his armour was badly buckled, and it was clear he needed help quickly.

"Help me up," he gasped.

Taylor hoisted the Commander up with his left arm and gritted his teeth through the pain he felt soar through his body. He could barely support the Commander who was laying most of his weight down on the Major. Mitch looked to Jafar who stood awaiting his orders.

"Give the Commander a hand," stated Taylor.

The creature quickly responded and rushed to Kelly's side, simply hoisting him up as if he weighed no more than a child.

"The flag!" Kelly murmured.

Taylor crouched down and lifted the flag onto his shoulder and braced it with his broken arm, despite the pain.

"We've got just a few metres left, and I'll be damned if we aren't gonna make it now!" Taylor shouted.

They continued on towards the roof access chamber. Taylor could feel his body was a wreck once more, and he was thankful Jafar was taking the weight of the Commander, as he was barely able to support him. They reached the access doors and stepped through into the chamber. The interior doors clamped down, and they instantly felt gravity lessen which took the pain and pressure off them all.

"This is it. You won your war, Major, and today we win ours," Kelly said.

He reached forward and winced in pain as he hit the door exit button. The heavy double doors swung back before them, and they stepped out onto a small platform. It had a ladder that led to the very highest point in the colony. Jafar lifted Kelly onto his shoulder and hauled him up with Taylor close behind.

Pulses of light and tracer still lit up the sky above them, but far less than they had seen on their descent. They reached the top of the steps and staggered out across the rooftop to where the flag used to stand. All that was left was a snapped mast where the enemy had torn it down. Kelly dragged himself up and took the flag from Taylor. He used it to support his weight as he limped to the post. Finally, he turned back to look at their fleet and stretched upright, holding the flag with pride.

* * *

General Schulz had been watching the progress of the battle over several display screens on the bridge of his vessel when it suddenly caught his eye.

"What the hell is that? Focus on that for me."

The Navy officer quickly zoomed in on the scene, and Schulz looked in astonishment at the moving sight. The officer quickly tapped a key and displayed it on the main monitor for all on the bridge to see. At first, several looked confused at the sight of the two men and the alien atop the building. But the reason quickly sank in.

"They've done it!" one shouted.

Cheering rang out across the vessel. Schulz turned to his comms officer.

"Send word to the fleet. Mission accomplished! The Moon is ours!"

On the rooftop of the Parliament building, Kelly turned to Taylor and reached out his hand in friendship.

"I never thought I'd see the day, Major, let alone to see you are the one here with me."

"I didn't do this alone, Sir."

Kelly nodded in agreement. He turned to the alien standing beside him.

"I didn't catch your name?"

"Jafar."

"I am in your debt. It will not be forgotten."

He reached out and shook the alien's hand that dwarfed his.

"This is a new dawn, Mitch. Humanity has taken back what is rightfully theirs. We have triumphed against all odds."

* * *

Chandra looked down at the bodies of fifteen soldiers that had fallen, and a medic who was desperately working to save two others. They were cutting down their enemy in vastly greater numbers, and yet they continued to come. Then when she was starting to doubt if they could win, Jackson's voice rang out.

"They're running! They're running!"

Chandra looked up to the ecstatic officer and rushed up to the edge of the defences to see for herself.

"My God, Kelly's done it," she whispered.

She turned back to the troops who were weary but in a

frenzy of excitement.

"I won't see one of those bastards escape this Moon. Kill them all!"

She lifted her rifle and leapt of the barricade, rushing forward and firing as she went. The troops screamed as they charged after her. An hour later, she was soaked in the enemy's blood and stood satisfied that she had done as they had promised. She had lost friends that day, but at least she could feel she had given better than they got. Jones rushed down the corridor to greet her, stopping in shock at the thick blue blood that was sprayed across her body and dripping from the Assegai in her hand.

"It's over, Chandra. We've won!"

* * *

Twenty minutes later, the troops of Inter-Allied lay about in the conference hall and surrounding rooms of the Parliament building. They had no idea where their lives went from there, but they were relieved. Eli lay stretched out in Taylor's arms. She was cut and bruised but felt better than ever.

The Colonel finally strode in to meet Taylor. She had wiped the enemy blood from her face, but it was stuck like glue everywhere else. She looked down at the two of them and smiled to see they had made it through. Jafar and Tsengal sat among the troops as they're own. They were engulfed in conversation with several of Taylor's marines.

"I guess they came through, then?" she asked.

"More than you can imagine."

A voice came over the tannoy throughout the whole colony. It was General Schulz.

"We have won a victory today of truly outstanding proportions. I want to thank every man and woman among you for your efforts. You have done everything that was asked of you and more. The invaders took humanity to the brink of destruction. Today we have clawed it back, and stand victorious!"

Cheers rang out and echoed all around the Parliament building."

"Today we reclaimed what was ours. Tomorrow, we take the fight to their lands!"

Clapping and cheering rang out. The thought of getting real payback was appealing to them all. But Taylor now knew one thing for sure; there was no end in sight to their war.

Defeating the enemy on Earth had ended the first Earth War. Invading the Moon had started the second.